CU00684482

Tales of Horror and the Unexplained

E.W. Bonadio

DEDICATION

To all the fans of Edgar Allen Poe, Stephen King and others that have thrilled or scared us with tales of terror and the macabre.

CONTENTS

Short Stories

Poetry

Black Aggie, a statue in a Baltimore cemetery. During the 50s urban legend surrounding this monument implied that if one sat on her lap at midnight, she would come alive and wrap her arms around the daring youth. Many of us teens visited but none dared to sit for very long on that cold hard statue's lap. Aggie now sits in a courtyard of some government building in Washington D.C.

Evolution of the Vampire Worm

Translucent skin stretched over a bulbous skeleton belied his true frailty. Ravaged by years of exposure to harsh other-world conditions, the stranger relied on physical deceptions and wit to walk among the unsuspecting earthlings. But as with all changelings in their most vulnerable state, the predator could not fully manage human perfection. It could not fully conceal the tell-tale pink folds surrounding the bulbous cranium, nor the strange acidic odor emanating from its pours. For some time, the long dormant creatures observed the colonists, listening, waiting, and strategizing on their plan for conquest. They mimicked speech patterns, languages and mannerisms, often chiming in on idle conversations without revealing themselves. But for most, the delicate balance of form and function proved a most challenging task.

The best the shape-shifter could do was to stay in the shadow as much as possible. Its natural body mass did not easily take to shifting into the larger and more muscular frames of earthlings. Some of the first to awaken had made fatal mistakes during the early years of the colonization. Although their attempts at infiltration failed miserably, those that followed learned how to adapt and move about undetected. This one now waiting in the shadows was clever. For nearly three weeks he had staked out his prey, learning her habits. He often tracked the victim from her habitat to the dig site. She worked late nearly every night and always traveled alone. It was just a matter of time when she would be in her most vulnerable state. Finally, the time had come to act and he was ready.

Dressed in a standard dark blue security services jumpsuit, the alien seemed a frumpy overfed earthling in ill-fitting clothes. His semi-bloated face pulsated with anticipation. With nearly lidless bulging eyes, he watched intently as the human contemplated her current situation. When certain that they were completely alone, he drew closer. It was very dark but the red glow of the Martian dunes reverberated onto the sky cloaking everything below in a dust covered rusty hue. A dome protecting humans from the extreme elements loomed far above the transit station that shuttled workers from base camp to the outlands and the Mars mining project where she worked. She would not be taking the shuttle. As a senior staff member, the human female had been given a personal source of travel, a NASA owned AUTO-BOT.

"You look lost young one. Can I be of assistance?" The alien had learned human speak well. With the ability to physically morph his organs into that of an earthling body with human vocal chords, the question completely disarmed the young woman.

Nev turned quickly around to face the strange character with piercing eyes.

"Oh, I'm not lost, just looking for a faster way to the recharging station." The stranger shrugged, at first not quite understanding her meaning.

"My BOT's nearly out of charge," she continued, "I need a quick charge."

Nearly empty, Nev's battery pack had run out of fuel and to get home she would need to get her BOT – battery operated transport - to the quick-charge center. Life in the 22nd century was no cakewalk for the volunteers working on NASA's Mars robotics project. With degrees in both computer technology and engineering, along with multiple skill sets in biomechanics, Nev eagerly signed on to put her skills to work assisting with the development of NASA's Mars-droid program. Then she would return back to Earth to marry her fiancé and love of her life, Bo.

"I can help," the strange looking security worker replied. Eagerly, he reached out and took her arm leading her over to a parked Mars rover. The sleek two-seat vehicle had massive back-up storage cells that allowed for safe travel outside the confines of the base. Turning abruptly, he jimmied a small hatch on the side of the rover. Moments later a three-meter long charging cord appeared in his hand. Looking around sheepishly, he unfurled it.

"Here, take this and plug it into your BOT. This machine is in full charge. It is quite capable of powering up your little BOT. " The stranger began nervously shuffling back and forth as if his feet hurt.

"Is that your Rover?" Nev asked quizzically. She suspected

not, but accepted the help. On Mars, security personnel were always cutting corners, appropriating power cells or charging units when necessary. Nev chuckled to herself thinking, I deserve to be docked for this, then quickly recovered asking,

"I appreciate the help but why are you so nervous?"

The strange little man thrust the cable into her hand. "Not nervous, just in a hurry. Time to eat soon…yes, I'm hungry and time to eat soon. Just wanted to help a fellow."

"Fellow?", she chortled. Nev began to suspect that the stranger may have been high on 'Martian gold', an illegal amphetamine based drug smuggled in from the Earth.

He quickly re-stated, "Fellow colonist I meant to say."

Nev was one of only a dozen or so specialists with a personal BOT but it had been the third time in a month that she had run low on a charge. The stranger watched intently as Nev went to work recharging the BOT's battery cell. Quickly, the meter on her vehicle climbed to nearly half full. "That's enough," she quipped with a wave of her hand. Nev unplugged the cord and handed it back to her little helper.

"Thanks, I appreciate your help. If there is anything I can do…"

But as he grabbed the cord Nev felt a strange sensation from below that began creeping up the pant leg of her jumpsuit.

"Now I will take payment." A thin whip-like appendage

appeared from behind the creature. It wrapped around her neck pulling her away from the BOT. The alien continued shifting back to its natural state and Nev froze as the metamorphosis continued. The transformation now complete it resembled a giant maggot, three sets of arms protruding from its mid section and a pulsating whiptail that coiled below. Nev understood that she was in serious trouble and she tried to scream. It was useless - she was utterly alone. It was the dreaded shape-shifting worm. Reports by base security assured the colonists that the situation under control. That was months before. The alien worms had learned from past mistakes and had revised their plans. They now only chose the most venerable women colonists, those that could be easily taken.

"No," she cried out as his body slithered forward. Nev could see the needle-like projection extending from its bloated belly. Like a large mosquito's feeding tube, the shaft found a vein and she felt a faint surge of alien blood coursing through her body, mingling with her own. The alien vampire had successfully infused her blood with his. The victim was now prepped for nightly feeding and it would visit her often, mingling its blood with hers. Nev was to provide more than just sustenance. She was now a means to the preservation of his species. She would not remember the encounter or the terror of that night, only the strange feeling of dread and the recurring metallic taste every time she ate or drank. Nev was special. The alien's blood had only slightly affected her motor skills. She was strong and the perfect specimen and her seed would be a leader.

The alien worms, a race of inter-galactic vampires, settled on Mars long before the first earth colonists arrived. After countless centuries of hibernation a proper host had come, human guinea pigs ripe for experiment. But their strategy was not to kill. Far worse, their goal was enslavement. In early tests their prey quickly fell into madness followed by a quick and agonizing death, but soon they learned to inject the proper doses of tainted alien blood. The earthling politicians knew of the threat but did little to stem the problem. The worms were a concern, but worth the risk when there was so much to be gained through off-world exploration.

Three months passed and Nev's encounter with the vampire seemed nothing more than a bad dream. Her daily activities revolved around work and sleep and Nev's eating habits diminished. She became slightly anemic and disinterested in social activities, but when she was told that her fiancé, Bo, was coming from Earth for a visit, she perked up. He had heard the stories of infected colonists and was concern for Nev's safety. During their first night together Bo noticed the changes.

"Are you feeling Ok?" he asked. "You've lost weight and your skin feels clammy. Then there is that strange smell each time you take a breath."

"Oh, so I'm anorexic and I have bad breath? I've been working very hard, that's all. Not getting much sleep lately."

"Well, let's not go there. I only meant..."

"Yes, you are just concerned," she quipped." Bo prodded, "I had hoped to keep you up late tonight but that might not be a good idea. You should go to the clinic tomorrow to check out these symptoms."

With a sudden burst of exuberance, Bo pleaded,

"Take some time off. We'll spend it together." Nev did not immediately respond. Her nervous system was beginning to shut down for the night, a reaction to the tainted blood and strange cerebral hold that the parasite had on her. Her eyes fluttered and began to close as she slurred out a response. "I don't know Bo...I'm tired now and…

Bo cut in quickly.

"I've missed you Nev. All this talk on Earth of alien infestations and… it just pushed me over the edge. Now I'm beginning to worry that you might have become infected."

Nev was trying to stay awake but her body would not cooperative. Bo stroked her shoulder. "I had to be here for you, Nev. I'm not leaving until you are released to return to Earth. After all, we are getting married."

Nev smiled thinly. Yawning deeply, she rolled over. Bo smiled back and patted her on the back of her head. "Get some sleep. I'm here to take care of you."

Nev slid into a deep coma-like state. She had always been a light sleeper and the change in both her demeanor and physical state worried the young earthling man. Bo sat for a few minutes watching the rise and fall of her chest. He stroked her long black hair. As he fumbled with her locks, he noticed a small red welt near the base of Nev's neck. It was a fresh wound and instinctively he searched her upper torso finding three additional spots. "Something's wrong here," he murmured to himself. "Nev's not well." He had seen it in her eyes before she fell off to sleep. He had noticed the cold clammy feel of her skin, and the lack of color in her face. News of the alien attacks had concerned him enough to make the trip. Bo was there to protect her and if that meant staying on Mars for the duration of her tour, he was willing to make the sacrifice.

Tired from the long trip to Mars, he wondered if his mind was playing games. There were unanswered questions, but Nev's fragile state had only heightened his concern and he decided to take her to the clinic the next morning for a check-up. To relieve the tension, Bo pulled out his recently purchased PIC-3, a miniature 3D audio/video device loaded with hundreds of video novels that could be played in virtual reality mode. Twenty minutes later he disengaged the device and popped a standard issue relaxation tablet. Within seconds the effects of the drug kicked in and he slept.

Nev's bedroom was a small space within the cubical comprising her living quarters. It was dark except for a pulsing white LED light over the equally small kitchen unit. An electronic flash oven situated over a pull down table hovered above a set of matching chairs. The first few hours passed uneventfully. Bo dreamed of married life on Earth, a new beginning for Nev and children, three or four little ones to keep them busy while others found pleasure and excitement exploring the universe. Arousing from a deep sleep, Bo suddenly detected a faint sulfuric smell much stronger than the odor coming from Nev's body. It burned Bo's eyes and he strained trying to adjust to the darkened interior. Once fully alert he noticed something strange, a shadowy mass in the corner of the unit. The alien was completing the change to its natural state and as it slithered free from its human garb, Bo reacted. Quickly, he sat up and looked around for a weapon. The parasite had returned to feed and did not expecting confrontation with a non-infected earthling. Briefly considered a hasty retreat. It was fully changed and could not readily morph back quickly so it advanced on the threat. Bo rolled the covers back to free his legs. His next thought was for the safety of Nev.

"Nev, wake up," Bo whispered. Shaking her gently he repeated the words, louder now, further inciting the worm. She did not respond. Nev's mind was clouded by a strange connection to the alien and its tainted blood. Her nervous system had shut down as it did each night allowing it to feed at will.

Bo rose up in bed and immediately the worm-like creature coiled. Defensively, it shifted into a cobra stance and sprang at the earthling. Its bloated body gyrated as snake-like appendages sprung out wildly, wrapping tightly around his legs. Now pinned to the bed, Bo squirmed frantically. From out of its soft underbelly, a short needle-like tube emerged thrusting powerfully towards Bo's throat. As it moved to strike Bo instinctively shoved his knee up to its mid-section. Temporarily gaining the upper hand, the young earthling took the slug's bulbous head in his hands. The vampire worm's beady eyes puffed out like an over inflated balloon and it hissed a faint plume of sulfuric acid into his face. As the worm strained against his grip its mouth opened to reveal multiple rows of sharp teeth. Suddenly, Bo felt a sharp prick from the worm's feeding tube. He recoiled, pushing back just before the alien could begin pumping the venomous nectar into his body.

"Ayah," he screamed and with a powerful burst of energy he thrust his right fist into the intruder's mouth. With a sharp snap and pop the vampire's face exploded and instantly a mixture of alien blood, gooey brain matter, and tissue splattered all over Bo and onto the floor. The worm was dead and Bo kicked it off quickly to free his legs.

"Nev, Nev, wake up."

The young woman woke from her stupor and instinctively grabbed her throat. "Oh, that dream, its come again," she cried out. Then she looked over at the carnage and gasped.

Bo knew immediately that its death had released her, the connection now broken between parasite and its host. The well-placed fist to the alien's head had saved Nev from a never-ending nightmare.

When fully recovered from the chaos, Bo called base security.

"I'm calling the medics also," he told Nev and reassured her with a kiss. PMT medical staff came swiftly to check them out and administer anti-venom serum. At the infirmary, they flushed out Nev's system and assured her that the alien infection was removed. Bo suffered a few bruises and a pulled muscle but no stab wounds or punctures could be found. Within a week, the young female specialist was back at work with a new project, loading program software for a massive robotic mining droid. Bo's recovery took longer. The effects of the sulfuric mist caused severe headaches and nausea but they subsided in time.

Bo's heroic stand had saved Nev from the alien vampire. But he worried that she would never fully recover from the exposure. She was free from the vampire but not the tinny smell. Within the year concern over the vampire matter subsided. There were other infestations but the bugs had all been destroyed. Life in the colony settled down and all infected humans were eventually tested negative for worm related maladies. The mundane existence of off-world living replaced alien paranoia and Bo eased into an off-world routine as safety and security officer in charge of their building. When Nev's projects concluded she signed off on her assignment paperwork and collecting a sizable bonus for a job well done. However, in her final physical, she learned of a change in her condition. Just prior to their scheduled departure for Earth, she happily informed her mate,

"I have great news Bo. You're going to be a father." Bo was stunned. "So soon? I thought that we decided to wait?"

"Yes, we did, but sometimes things like this just happen." She didn't know how or why, but Nev was happy to have conceived on Mars. "I had taken precautions," she said, "but that doesn't matter now. It's a boy, Bo, a boy"

Eight months later their son was born. They named him Conner. The baby arrived with unexpected attributes, superior motor skills, an ability to understand and mimic speech before he could sit up, and a full set of stiletto-like baby teeth by the end of his first month. No one noticed the small dart-like protrusion hidden between his left cheek and gum. Nev paid no mind to Conner's oddities, but by his fifth birthday his insatiable desire for drawing blood from schoolmates forced them into home schooling the boy.

By Conner's seventh birthday, three live-in nannies had mysteriously disappeared. Others had also vanished, victims of the boy's burgeoning lust for sustenance. But there was never any incriminating evidence against the child. In Conner's thirteenth year, Bo fell ill with a mysterious infection. Acute anemia followed and within three months he was dead. Nev's grief at the loss of her husband nearly destroyed her. Conner showed no sign of grief or sorrow. Nev feared that her son had a role in Bo's death and confronted the child.

"Son, do you know what happened to your father?"

"Yes mother, he died."

"I know, but how did he die?"

"Infection I suppose."

"And how did your father get this infection?"

"It was meant to be I guess. Mother, you are safe here with me. I won't let anything happen to you. Now please, let's not talk of death. This Earth is a new world to conquer and I plan on doing just that."

Nev decided not go to the authorities for fear of setting off a witch hunt. He was her son and the only link to Bo. After Bo's death, Conner began to shut himself away, breaking from both friends and family. That changed as Nev began to see the physical changes in her son. He was turning into a man, not wholly human, but something other than an earthling. Then they began to come to the house, first one then others, always alone but never during the day. After a dozen such meetings, Conner came to Nev.

"Mother, you must prepare for the coming change. There is a new way, a new life for those on earth and you've got to be ready to accept it." Nev asked,

"Who are those strangers you have been meeting with?"

"Friends mother...brothers not of this Earth. The last has told me, I am to be the one."

"The one?"

"Yes, I have been chosen. I will be the leader of the coming revolution. But we must wait. We are not yet physically ready. You should be proud mother, when we have taken control of earth, I will return to Mars to collect the brethren."

"I always knew that you were special," she said unconvincingly. A sinking feeling overtook Nev and she feared for the future, not for herself but for her world. A flashback came to her and she remembered the encounter with the worm. It was clear that somehow, her son was a product of that encounter.

A few days later Conner disappeared. He was not alone.

The phenomena of teenage children disappearing occurred dozens of times in many cities around Earth. Grieving families gave up hope of ever finding them and police departments closed most cases as runaways. Then the plague hit and unexpectedly people began to die from viral infections similar to what Bo experienced before his death. Calls went out for an investigation into the epidemic and all previous Martian colonists were requested to report for further testing. After receiving her notice, Nev stepped forward with what she believed was happening on Earth. Hoping that she was not too late, she sounded the alarm. The alien worms had infiltrated Earth. In their new form they no longer needed to be shape-shifters. She concluded that the mass of missing boys and girls were actually the spawn of vampire worms from Mars.

Some twenty years after the spate of alien infections, the progeny of the alien birth mothers had fully matured. A new race of beings, humanoid-alien vampires emerged. They had come of age to breed and feed on Earthlings. A young man named Conner was their leader. Along with his brethren, Conner moved in earnest to begin the subjugation of humanity. The seed of a few score of colonists tainted by the blood of vampire worms now challenged humans for dominance over the earth's creatures. They were stronger and more resilient than their predecessors, a flawed race of sinister galactic grubs. More importantly, their genetically altered bodies became the consummate evolutionary upgrade. Their goal had always been the evolution of the species. In their present form, the vampire worms seemed to have no equal. Nev would become their Earth mother, a queen and the source of renewal for a new generation of galactic vampires. They would come often in homage to feed from the mother's blood of Conner, the first-born and savior.

THE END

The Ghost of Merrick Mansion

Before that day twenty years ago, I had never really believed in ghosts. My perspective changed however, when I came face to face with the ghost of Merrick mansion.

It all began on a late afternoon and a lazy summer's day in front of a deserted Victorian house adorned with stained glass windows, high turrets, and gargoyles. Those strange gargoyles were the catalyst in my becoming a true believer. A curious boy with attitude topped off by a smidge of naivety, I thought my life charmed. Having heard the stories of haunted houses and graveyards, I yearned to feel the rush of playing hide and seek with mythical creatures of the night. The exhilaration of late night prowling quickly became addictive. Not into destructive behavior, the prime motive in my addiction was pushing the envelope – to live dangerously. Scribbling chalk graffiti on tombstones and mausoleums was certainly not out of bounds. Neither was breaking into the Merrick place.

Merrick mansion had been deserted for nearly ten years. It was also the center of several mysterious happenings, one being the accidental death of the young man who lived there and his widowed mother a week after his funeral. A short walk from my friend, abode, the Merrick place had seen it's best days. We called it a mansion because of the many strange adornments gracing the exterior. Funny grotesque creatures, tongues hanging out, a perfect perch for starlings. I imagined those devilish creatures gulping down any who lingered. Nestled at the end of the street some forty yards from the thoroughfare, it sat unadorned and in disrepair. To young Turks like Benny and I, the Merrick place was a mystery mansion with many secrets waiting to be revealed.

Benny Scarfo, and I were not bad eggs, but on occasion we did go overboard, like the time we planted a cherry bomb in old man Gifford's mailbox. That gimmick cost me a month's allowance. After a forced penance, community service and a serious grounding, Benny suggested that we cool it with the neighbors. "Let's break into the Merrick place," he offered, "it's deserted and we can't get into trouble just rooting around." He paused, "But I heard it's haunted."

"Haunted, with ghosts?" I said.

"That's what my dad said, but I think he just wanted to scare me away from exploring the place. Told me that a kid got hurt trying to climb into the second story window to retrieve a baseball a year ago...said a ghost tried to pull him into the house."

"Then it must be true," I cautioned.

"It would be fun to find out," Benny answered. "I know a

way in. Maybe we'll find hidden treasure." I cringed at the thought decided to meet him there at dusk. Standing at the front gate of the driveway leading up to an oversized portico, Benny rubbed his palms. "This will be the best adventure ever...look at those carvings over the windows. They look like dragons."

"No, they're gargoyles," I offered. I was well versed in such things, having read up on the devilish carvings in medieval history class. I reminded him, "They were originally put onto buildings to ward off evil spirits."

"Cool," he drooled, "then one of them can protect us from the ghost. I'm gonna get me one."

I cringed. "No Benny, I don't think that's a good idea."

"Oh, so you're scared of a little carving? Not me. I want one and if you don't help me, I'll do it alone."

"Okay," I said. "I'm in, but the gargoyles are high up and you'll have to crawl out from the attic. Hope you're not afraid of heights," I cautioned. Benny grimaced and after a minute of silence, he pointed and said,

"That window just below that attic vent. We'll get one from there. I'll bring the tools." As Benny chatted away I stared up at the tower and the creatures hanging above the window facing the side yard. Then I saw it, a flicker of light. Faint at first, it moved left to right midway across the window. I grabbed at Benny's sleeve. "There's someone up there, Benny...someone's in the window."

He was surveying the grounds and as he turned the light was gone. "Nah, it's probably your imagination. You're just spooked. My dad says that old lady Merrick died in that room up there." He pointed to the tower jutting out from the side of the house. "Others have said she was kooky...said that she died of a broken heart over her son's sudden death… willed the property to the city." He shook his head. "Nobody cared about old lady Merrick. But there were whispers that she and her husband were very superstitious…dabbled in the occult."

A young couple rounded the corner and I turned away. Paying no attention, they walked past us, lost in each other. "That's Mr. Boggs's son Jimmy with his new girlfriend," Benny said. "He lives next door."

"Hope he didn't hear us," I chirped.

"Nah, don't worry, Jimmy's cool," he answered. "Right now he's got his mind on girls… get's a new one every month." Benny smiled. "I've got a hunch he'll stick with this one for awhile…she's hot."

I was spooked but Benny assured me, "It's just your imagination."

"Okay, Benny," I conceded, "what time tonight?"

"Eleven-thirty. Can you slip out that late?"

"Yeah, eleven-thirty." We'd agreed to meet under the street light near the front gates. Then, when all was clear, we'd slip around to the side gate between the Boggs house and Merrick place. Benny assured me, "There is a row of large cypress trees that will hide us. Once we jump the gate, it will be smooth sailing."

At exactly eleven-thirty I rounded the corner and waited under the light. It was quiet except for the summer breeze rustling errant tree limbs lining the street. After a few minutes alone, I began to have second thoughts. I felt like a grave robber. Benny was late but after fifteen minutes of pacing he arrived, sweating heavily. "What happened?" I asked.

"Almost got caught climbing out my bedroom window. It

squeaked as my dad walked past my room. I jumped back into bed just before he checked on the noise."

"Whew," I said, shaking my head. "I was just about to leave…thought you chickened out."

"Nah, not me," he sniffled catching a dribble of snot on his sleeve, "I'm no chicken."

I laughed. "Yeah, I guess not, but I still have a funny feeling about this." Looking up at the tower window, a shiver ran up my spine and I felt the urge to piss my pants. Up above, one the gargoyles had shifted. It was now looking directly at us, its tongue hanging to the side, not straight as I had remembered earlier.

"Look Benny" I said, "doesn't that gargoyle look different to you now?" Benny gazed up scratching his head. "No, now let's get going." He dragged me along by the arm and as we reached the side gate my blood raced. The excitement of the caper took hold and adrenaline pumped furiously into all parts of my body. A sudden breeze chilled my bones adding to the mysterious feel of the adventure. Once inside the grounds, Benny quickly covered the distance to the side door. I followed behind, less confidently, aware of every shadow in the yard. It was late at night and no credible reason for someone to be hiding in the bushes or behind a tree, but my mind began to play tricks.

As I caught up to Benny, he was jimmying the door. It opened and I remarked, "You're a pro at this, Benny." He turned and smiled. Once in the house, we found the kitchen a mess. Empty beer bottles, plastic bags, and cigarette butts were strewn everywhere. "Looks like we missed the fun," Benny whispered. "There's been a beer party and the slobs never bothered to clean up."

"Yeah, I guess so," I whispered. "Watch yourself, you don't want to get cut on broken glass." Benny didn't respond and went about his business looking for the stairway up to the third floor. As we climbed the stairs, creaks and groans followed every step. The circular stairway with its ornate banister showed its age. Halfway up the second flight one of the stairs treads gave way and Benny's left foot fell through. Briefly panicked, I raced up to help. "That was a scare," he chuckled. "Okay, now who's scared?" I asked.

At the top of the second flight, the hallway stretched out in two directions. Benny knew exactly which way to go, darting down the right corridor. I followed behind, my eyes glancing around. There were four doors on each side and at its end, the hallway turned to the right. "This is it," Benny said, but I temporarily lost him when he made the turn. "Benny," I called. "Benny, are you there?" There was no response and as I made it to the corner, I froze. "Boo!" Benny's hands reached out and grabbed at me. Behind him, a whiff of dust appeared and I gasped, "Ayah!" Benny's reaction was swift. "Shhhh!" We were now just a few feet from the tower room and my companion was giddy. From the knapsack on his back Benny pulled out a hammer and cooed, "This is going to be easy. Now let's get to it. We've gotta find the attic stairs."

From my position in the hallway, I peered into the tower room. The door was open and an eerie light filtered into the hallway. I exclaimed, "See, the light? I told you that there was a light in that room earlier."

"Yeah" he answered, "but it's just the moonlight. Now quiet down and follow me." He pulled out his flashlight and searched along the ceiling. "Ah, here it is," he said. It was a trap door with a pull cord. "Now get on my shoulders and grab the cord."

Reluctantly, I obliged. As I grabbed the rope and pulled, the door opened. The track slid down and a built-in ladder glided to the floor. "Yes," Benny exclaimed, and he bent over to ease me back to solid ground. The doorway to the attic was secure, but the black hole above seemed to go nowhere. Benny flashed his light up into the darkness. There was a scurrying above and Benny turned to me. "Rats?"

"Got me," I answered. "First one up's gotta chase them away," he proclaimed. "Be my guest," was all I could think to say.

Benny took charge, climbing up the ladder. Once up he called back, "Not rats, just pigeons roosting. We scared the piss out of them."

My fear subsided. Ever since I saw the movie, Ben I feared rats and I chuckled, thinking to myself, Ben - Benny? I followed more confidently then when we first arrived. Benny was first to the attic vent. He opened it, testing his weight on the round circular slatted fixture. Held at the pivot point by a half-inch metal rod, it swung easily. "That's how the pigeons get in," he said, pushing the vent up and down on the swivel. "Smart birds," I quipped. "Flying rats," he snarled back. "Got bird doo on my jacket sleeves. Okay, get over here and watch. I'm gonna slide onto the vent. Now when I get halfway out, hold onto my legs." I did as instructed. It was a cinch and on the first try Benny called out to me,

"Okay, I got it, now pull me in." As I slid his legs back onto the floor of the attic, I noticed the gargoyle. It was about eight inches wide and twelve inches long. Benny had pulled it off the dowel attaching it to the corbel. The whimsical face temporarily held me spellbound and suddenly I wanted one for myself. There was another out there within his reach. Benny asked, "Want one?"

Shaking off the temptation, I decided, "No, no thanks. I'm not going out there." Benny laughed. "I'll do it. They pull off easy. The wooden dowel holding it was all cracked. It popped right off."

Something inside told me to get out of there. I didn't understand why, but my gut began to churn. I was feeling sick and the gargoyle's face only made the dread worsen. As Benny cradled the carving in his hand he felt strangely emboldened. "Well if you don't want the other one, I'll take it for myself and have a pair of 'em for my bookshelf." He turned, placing the carving on the floor and again slid onto the vent, this time more confident than ever. "I don't need your help," he called back, "Just watch."

Suddenly, I could tell that something was wrong. Benny began breathing hard and his legs squirmed as if he was struggling to get free from the vent. On the floor, the gargoyle's mouth began to change. It was moving, laughing now, and the uncurled tongue began to curl upward. I grimaced and backed away, hollering out to Benny, "What's going on?" Inside, his feet flailed about as he tried to grab onto the sides of the vent. Then he called back, "Something's pulling me out." I looked over the top and noticed a rope-like whiff of smoke. It held onto Benny's free hand. In the other, the second gargoyle's face changed. Its brow furrowed and the expression changed from whimsical to serious. I yelled, "Put it back," and I grabbed his legs. "Put it back, Benny," I screamed. Looking through the vent, I saw that he had not yet replaced the gargoyle. The creepy band of smoke still held firm. Gnarled fingers of smoky sinew crawled up his arm. Another wisp of smoke appeared out of the night and a grotesque demon head appeared. It wailed like a banshee straining mightily in an attempt to pull him through the vent. "Hold onto me," he screamed, "and don't let go." I tried, but my strength was no match for the powerful demon. Its bright red eyes gleamed in the dark and I feared that Benny was about to get his neck broken over an old wooden carving.

Just as I began to lose my grip I saw the reflection of a light flickering against the attic ceiling. It was the same light that I noticed from the street hours before. The candle, held by the ghost of old lady Merrick, illuminated the attic space. Her shadow loomed above and I turned to face the threat. She approached her face milky white and dour. A high-necked nightgown flowed from around her translucent body. Disapprovingly, she frowned and shook her head as if to scold me for the intruding onto her property. I was a mere mortal, just a petty thief violating her home and I now feared for my own life. Benny was now nearly three quarters out of the vent. In moments, he'd be laying dead three stories below us.

"Help us," I screamed. Her face brightened, but she did not reply. I pleaded with the vision from the spirit world. "Please won't you help us?" My personal fear was overshadowed by the need for someone to help Benny, even if it was a ghost. He was in trouble and I could no longer manage to hold on. The demon holding him had evil intent and I turned back to the vent, tears streaming down my face. "Help me save my friend," I cried. Time was running out and the apparition did not seem to care. Her first intention was to scold me, "You two have come here to steal from me. Why should I help?" Quickly, I answered, "I know about your boy…sorry for your loss." There was a sudden change and she softened. "Yes, my poor son, he rests now with his father."

She breezed past me, her arm reaching out for Benny's right leg. "Now let go," she said and I obliged. My hand released and it brushed against her gown. The icy cold took me and panic ensued. I began to get up to run, but she held me back.

"You cannot not leave your friend," she demanded. Benny was in grave danger, a demon pulling on him from one side of the vent and a ghostly lady tugging at the other. "Let him go you damned demon," I cursed. The ghost's grip tightened around Benny's leg and I could see that she was getting the upper hand. "Be gone from here," she commanded and the craggy fingers of the demon released.

Suddenly, the demonic aggressor gave way and faded into the night. Benny's body went limp but she held onto his legs. Slowly, the ghostly apparition brought Benny's listless body back into the attic. She laid him on the floor. Bending over, she touched his brow. A comb appeared and she ran it once through his hair. Placing the candle on the floor, she picked up Benny's stolen gargoyle. Her milky white body drifted through the attic wall and her hand affixed the gargoyle back onto its corbel. Flowing back into the attic space, she came to me. Her lips moved and I could not hear her speak, but the words formed in my head.

"My friends out there keep evil away from this house. My husband George had them added to protect us from the evil ones that prowl in the night. Demons have no power inside this house as long as the watchers keep guard." She gave me a smile. "Now take your friend and leave." Then she vanished. The candlelight flickered and everything went dark. Benny groaned and began to stir, but I heard a noise below us, first a bang, then footsteps coming up the stairs. My heart pounded heavily and I supposed that other ghostly figures were coming now to evict us. "Benny, Benny, get up," I whispered loudly. "We've gotta get outta here." He groaned again and then sat up. "What happened?" He could not remember getting stuck out on the attic vent and had no recollection of the demon that had him in its grip. All that he remembered was pulling off the first gargoyle and going out to get the second one.

"Where, where's my carving?" he stammered. "Forget it, Benny, let's go," I pleaded. The noise of the footsteps grew louder and as we finished our climb down the attic stair, I felt a hand on my shoulder. "Gotcha!" It was Jimmy, the older boy from next door. "What are you two kids doing here? This house is off limits, now let's go." I was glad to see a living human being and said,

"That old Mrs. Merrick told us to get out and we're getting out all right."

He laughed, "So you've seen old lady Merrick? I've often wondered if anyone else noticed her in the window." He began walking us down the stairs. "My bedroom faces the side yard and the tower room. Sometimes at night I can see her walking around, a candle in one hand and a comb in the other. My dad says that it's just my imagination, but I still look for her every night. Say, what were you two doing here anyway?"

Benny was still coming out of his stupor so I answered,

"We tried to steal the gargoyles outside the attic vent. When Benny snatched the second one, he…he got stuck. I tried to pull him back, but it was old lady Merrick that saved him. Then she said to leave."

As we walked out of the house, Jimmy teased, "I guess that you'll have a great bedtime story to tell your children someday when you're all grown-up." Looking up at the tower, I thought I caught the faint glow of a lighted candle. "Yeah," I said, "some bedtime story."

I don't think that Jimmy Boggs believed me, but that's of no consequence now. I learned a valuable lesson from the apparition at Merrick mansion. And the moral of this little story is clear - Evil lurks in wait for every fool, be it the wayward thief or that of a youthful prankster. The demon that I saw pulling my friend out of the vent may have been a figment of my imagination, but as for ghosts, I only know this...it's always nice to have one on your side.

THE END

The Road to Peril

On the road to peril's gate

near the darkest hour of night

a traveler came upon the count

of seven murdered souls

stacked much like cord wood

in a gully below the ridge.

Their twisted torsos sickened him.

It was uncommon fear,

that strange sensation

of rushing blood cells

through tightened arteries

and a lump in the throat

that drove him to investigate.

It also foreshadowed his fate.

He strove to understand

the method of their demise

and to reason within reality

justification for such violence

against those unwitting victims

left to whither in the elements.

Did the killer lurk nearby, he wondered?

Turning slowly around

he spied the perpetrator

looming near to strike

with that ancient weapon

set high like an elephant's tusk

its stiff blade bearing down.

He turned to run from death's door.

Too late he realized

as a blow to his arm

clove flesh near the bone

and in sudden desperation

he turned to make a stand

or by the attempt, perish.

It was then that fear turned to rage.

Rage, that sudden rush

of uncontrolled madness

coursed through his being

and with unbridled resolve

he met head on in combat

the assassin's next assault.

Swiftly, he parried the next blow.

With the strength of ten

he disarmed the nameless killer

and turned the tide against him

using the cruel weapon's blade

to bludgeon the highwayman

with a series of short swift blows.

The victim had bested his assailant.

As his rage subsided

he felt energized by the effect

of this chance encounter

and the rush of power

never before experienced

either in thought or in deed.

He became lost in a world of death.

The evil weapon embraced him

and returning to the bodies

he surveyed the handy work

with a new sense of respect

for the instrument of death

now in his possession.

He imagined each murder as his own.

Greedily, he snickered

as the blood stained halberd

cut through the air

longing to skewer again

any adversary worthy

of its newfound master.

He longed to rekindle that feeling.

The madness had taken him

to the nighttime shadows

where he watched and waited

for a next unsuspecting soul

to finish that which was started

by the highwayman on the road.

One more, number nine for the night.

E.W. Bonadio

The Grave of Armond Balosteros

The young soldier, a traveler from a city near the northern coast of Spain, plodded through the ancient cemetery, searching for the burial place of a long dead relative. The graveyard lay near a line of stony battlements, part of Spain's defenses against the French during Napoleon's invasion nearly a century before. As he wandered among the monuments a morning chill cut through his half-opened woolen jacket. Flinching from the biting cold, his hand squeezed the estate document confirming the internment. A hero, the account proclaimed, of the Spanish in their fight against the French. Continuing his quest, the young man searched each stone and statue looking for the familiar family coat of arms adorning the monument.

It had been a long and arduous journey. With each step over the hard rocky ground the soldier's calf muscles ached. Stopping near an oak tree, he found rest on a random headstone. It angled slightly from many years of settlement and nature's abuse. After a brief test of its sturdiness he straddled the stone, bent over and attempted to read aloud the name "ARM...." He brushed away debris to finish, but a chill wind rushed through the trees peppering his face. Long dead oak leaves flew up and around the gravesite, and as they whirled about the gravesite, he stirred. Above the din, the soft and remarkably elegant voice of a man caught his ear.

"Winter comes early, does it not?"

Bemused, the young man turned to greet the stranger, but the cemetery was empty; he was utterly alone.

The voice came again, this time in the traditional hail of olden times.

"Greetings gentle stranger! I was not expecting a visitor on such a bleak autumn morn. It pleases me that you stopped here to rest your bones." Startled, the young man froze in place, listening though not yet understanding the nature of the voice, nor its intention.

"Forgive the ghastly appearance of this stony ground; the years have been less kind to those of us who share the confines of this place. Are you lost or simply searching for a kin from early times?"

After surveying the ground near the stone, the soldier relaxed his guard pondering the question. He thought to solicit the voice on the placement of his kin; however, the uncertainty overruled action. After a short reprieve, the voice revealed its unseen persona and true intentions.

"My name is Armond Balosteros. Long have I been interred in this desolate place. Your attention to my fateful story is welcome, so if I may be so bold, please humor me and stay awhile."

Weary from his journey and too confused to challenge his own senses, the soldier considered the offer. It was obviously a daydream, possibly the effects of a recently emptied flask of brandy. "Perhaps it is just my imagination and the effects of the cold," he mused. Sitting back in stoic silence against the tilted headstone, he closed his eyes as the storyteller began his tale.

"It was on a mild September morning that my fate was sealed by the length of a hangman's rope. This severe punishment coincided with a broken friendship caused by the course of unfortunate historical events. You see, a friend tainted by life's reversals, offered his assistance. In the end betrayal was his game. I entrusted my most cherished possessions to this so-called friend. However, it was not my land, buildings, livestock and earthly staples. They were forfeit to the state. My chief concern was the safeguarding of my children. Their security was to be secured by the preservation of my family's hidden heirlooms and a sizable stash of coin.

I must now persist in exposing this treachery and how within a few days of judgment my friend contrived to steal my wealth. As an act of trust, I placed my holdings with a man from the coast named Rodrigo. I myself hailed from Salamanca. Rodrigo and I shared schooling in Madrid, two lads sent into the care of the Jesuits. Our fathers were wealthy landowners and as part of the privileged class, it was required that we should pass into manhood with the rudiments of discipline and culture. We received all that the church had to offer in the way of Christian salvation. However, with the unfortunate passing of my father, I returned home and took over the management of the estate. Two seasons hence my mother passed on, dying of consumption which left me sole heir of the estate. Alone at the age of twenty-six and longing for companionship, I chose to take a wife.

From all corners, fathers and clergy offered widows and daughters to share my bed in marital bliss. I rejected most candidates as being either amazingly dimwitted or too portly for my liking. Nevertheless, a local commoner, a wistful farm girl named Esmeralda caught my eye. Against the railings of many elitist friends, we married and within a year, a beautiful daughter was born. Three years hence, my son arrived kicking and screaming his way into the world. Unfortunately, his birth was not without complication which led to a decline in Esmeralda's health. Not quite thirty, she developed a sickness that left her unable to manage the household. However, she had bore me two fine children and their affection for each other and their mother made me proud."

The young officer stirred as another gust of wind blew leaves into his face. Now longing to know more, he repositioned himself and pleaded with the voice, "Do continue sir, whoever you may be. You seem to have captured me in this dream and I am loath to retreat from it." The voice continued, now more assured of a ready ear from his guest.

"Now prior to my son's twelfth birthday, Rodrigo came to see me. With him was a most surly, adventurous looking patriot from the coast. Rodrigo and the man explained that it was my duty to join in resisting Napoleon's incursion into Spain. Being a simple agrarian and a practitioner of non-violence, I waved off any such involvement. It was at that very moment that I made a fatal mistake. I had misjudged Rodrigo's heart. Informed that Rodrigo's family had entrusted their estate to the cause, they now desired my property and stores as well. I bid them to stay with me in counsel until I could consider all options.

Three days passed and the men continued to ply me with grape and stories of French atrocities in my homeland. At the third evening meal, my son enlisted himself into our discussions. Being an impressionable lad, he could not hold back from interjecting himself on the other side of my opinion. With the odds now stacked against me I succumbed, agreeing that my land and stores could be used to sustain the rebels."

Again the young officer stirred, further intrigued by the course of the story. "I pray you sir, do continue as I long for an ending be it grim or not. Please, spirit, whether in my head or naught, finish the tale." Armond accepted the young man's plea and pressed on with his story.

"Now I come to a twist in the tale. In an effort to mire the French in an untenable position, the English sent Wellington into Portugal. From there he advanced into Spain and against them in force. Napoleon's eye had turned east towards Russia, and he failed to consider his nemesis. However, a great battle between Wellington's force and one of Napoleon's most accomplished generals, Marshal Marmont, soon improved Spain's fate. While Napoleon was forging towards Moscow through Borodino, the French prepared to meet the English near the city of Salamanca.

Just two days before the battle, Rodrigo and his friend appeared at my estate. They soon left to scout the terrain to the east, leaving shortly before the French arrived.

That next day the French general positioned his army at the crest of a ridge overlooking my estate. Having abandoned the town of Salamanca to the fast approaching English, Marmont was determined to make a stand on ground of his own choosing. As fate would have it, the French found three patriots retrieving munitions on my land. They turned me in for mercy's sake, thus avoiding the gallows. Summoned to the French commander, I explained that I had no choice but to allow my fellow citizens the use of my land and provisions. For that, the French charged me with sedition. On the behalf of my sickly wife and children, the commander reconsidered and granted me reprieve on the condition that I expose my hidden stores. In return for my life and for the safety of my family, I agreed.

Forthwith, I accompanied an officer and a few of his men to the hidden storage barns. Upon returning me home, my son overheard the French officer thank me for my help in procuring sorely needed supplies. Subsequently, upon my release, I moved the children east to the river Algabete, then north to the river Tormes. There I kept them out of harms way. My wife, too ill to travel, remained at the estate and under the care of my manservant.

Two days hence, the outcome was at hand. The English had bested the French and all seemed safe again, therefore, I returned home. I found my land sorely scorched and broken with the corpses of dead French and English soldiers still on the field. Upon inquiring about my wife and manservant, I came to find that they perished during the initial cannonades. Then at sundown, Rodrigo arrived. He came upon me with great pride in his heart boasting,

"The French are retreating. This will prove to be the turning point for us in Spain." At the site of my son, still distraught over his mother's death, the patriot grabbed the boy and hugged him saying,

"Don't cry young man, someday you too shall serve and we shall fight the enemy together". Dismayed, I grabbed my son from his arms and shouted him down.

"No Rodrigo, I will not have my son meet the same fate as his mother and my servant. Death is forever. I will not lose my son to such useless work."

However, in a fit of temper and grief, my boy struck back.

"But father, you gave provisions to the French. I heard the French captain thank you for leading them to the hidden stores. But for your misguided help of the enemy, my mother lies in her grave."

My jaw dropped at those words. They were as a dagger thrust into my heart. The silence of a thousand stares befell me, as I stood immobilized by that brief inquisition. My first thought was to pass it off as a slight misunderstanding; however, the gravity of the moment became clear. In a fit of anger, Rodrigo grabbed the hilt of his sword and a patriot pulled a pistol from his belt. I could not defend against my son's words but said my piece.

"To spare my life and assure the safety of my children, I gladly gave the stores to the French. It was for that purpose alone that I conceded them. After all, did I not do the same for you when asked, and did you not so win the day?"

Rodrigo pushed down the muzzle of the patriot's gun, and took my arm. We walked away from prying ears and once distanced from the others he said, "This was a great victory for our country but it may yet go ill for you my friend." He asked me to consider his next words very carefully.

"I must be frank with you Armond. I have lost most of my fortune to this war. However, you have placed yourself in more danger than I could ever hope to repeal. I am a leader in Spain's resistance, and your foolishness has caused me much shame. For aiding the French in this battle, a traitor's noose may be your fate, but it is in my power to protect you remaining loved ones. If you will tell me where your heirlooms and coin are concealed, I will hold them safe and entreat those in power to pardon you. If unsuccessful, I will acquire the best legal mind to advocate for you at trial. This I promise, if you will trust in me."

I was speechless. His every utterance hung on me like a stone. One by one, they weighed me down until a grotesque mask of self-pity covered my face. I protested again,

"I was only trying to save myself from a similar fate at the end of a French noose." Rodrigo was sympathetic but reformed his words.

"No my friend, I cannot promise anything, but you are about to be taken into custody. Look, they are forming to take you as we speak."

I turned back to the patriot. Three men in arms now stood by his side. I broke down, knowing that it was time to make the ultimate sacrifice for my children. I made Rodrigo swear that should it go badly for me, he should take in my children and care for their education and well-being. The pledge was enough to free me of my secrets. I looked over to the sweet faces of my children. Then I told Rodrigo where to find the heirlooms."

The young soldier, aghast at this latest revelation, braced himself to hear the balance of Armond's tale. He feared that poor Armond might have some unresolved commitment to revenge from the grave. However, the soldier did not believe that Armond's tale had an ending of consequence for him. Staring out towards the battlements he nervously asked, "Is there much more to this tale, sir? I am growing quite anxious."

Armond laughed. "I hope that you were not frightened by the second act. It's telling was an important prelude to the final chapter. I have weighed every word so that the story is clear. If my sensibilities about war and doing right by my family seem foolish, forgive me. I was no fool. I have no remorse or guilt, especially for the predicament that preceded my death. Whence the story comes full circle, I promise to give you an ending worthy of understanding."

The soldier nodded again, this time less certain of Armond's meaning.

"As you expect, the trial did not go well for me. However, sharing my jail cell was a gypsy elder. He had relieved an Englishman of his coin, a fate judged much less severe than my own. As they paraded him into my cell, he winked. Then he came over and squatted down near my makeshift bed. Smiling a near toothless smile, he sought out my name.

"Your name friend and your fate if it pleases you to tell... I am a curious old man who seeks company."

I could see that he craved conversation. As I related the story of my incarceration, he frowned. At each mention of Rodrigo's name, I could tell that he disapproved, but I continued to affirm our great friendship. As I spoke, the old man remained transfixed. After recounting a condensed version of recent events, I spoke of prideful things, my wife and our children. Nevertheless, I felt as if the old man was extracting tiny bits of my life and examining them for some unknown purpose. Our conversation ended on that pleasantry and I fell quiet.

Weary from the day's events, I fell asleep. During my rest, I drifted into a dream. Oddly, considering my impending doom, it was a pleasant one. I dreamt of lounging with my family on a riverbank. The children played and my wife held my hand. She kissed me and we laughed. It was a pleasant delusion, and when I awoke, the sweet memory of that dream remained. At mid-day, a meal consisting of lentils, bread and water was brought in by the guard – my last meal in the world of the living. I felt a tug at my sleeve; it was the old gypsy. He begged me,

"Share your bread with me, sir and I will pray for you."

In pity, I obliged. Besides, food no longer held any pleasure. The horror of the gallows and fear of heaving my meal before the hangman greatly concerned me. I drank in silence, sipping the tepid water from my dirty wooden cup. When the gypsy finished his feast of bread he came to me and said,

"Even now, placed before the gallows, you saw to care for another in need. For this, I will help you. We gypsy folk have certain gifts. That is why we are both feared and despised. However, I cannot keep you from the gallows kind master. That it is not in my power. This Rodrigo has betrayed you, and even now, he plots to send your children away in bondage. As you sit here espousing his friendship, your jewels are being weighed and appraised."

My mind was on the children; I cared not for the jewels and coin. Then, as if reading my mind he said,

"I can see to your children's safety. I can also grant you the curse of revenge. Will you have it?"

What could I lose? I chose to listen as he explained further. He asked me to decide if I wished my children to have happy lives or rich lives. I chose the first of his words. The old gypsy then asked their names and the location of Rodrigo's temporary residence. I told him it was at my very house. Picking up a fistful of dirt, the old man went to the cell's window and whispered to a dark presence on the other side. I wondered who had been there and for what purpose, but I dared not ask. Picking up a handful of dirt, he tossed it into the air and mumbled a few unintelligible words.

Coming back, he assured me,

"Your children will be kidnapped by my clan. They will be taken to safety in the mountains and will live happily to the end of their days."

The revenge curse was next. I wanted Rodrigo to feel my pain and as I spoke those words the old man smiled, telling me that he had expected such a thought. However, his revenge was even more severe than I could have imagined. The plan was devilish in its simplicity and I laughed heartily as he detailed Rodrigo's fate. Placing his hand on my temple, he told me to say Rodrigo's name three times. Then he chanted the curse.

"From one's fear into the other...fly fear, into the man called Rodrigo." The next morning as the guards removed me from the cell, my eyes met the old gypsy. I nodded a goodbye, turned and followed the guards to the gallows.

It would be a quick death for me, but not so for Rodrigo. You see, the old gypsy knew of Rodrigo's weakness. Hidden in the recesses of my mind, he extracted it from my boyhood memories.

Rodrigo had a penchant for sleep, enjoying long nighttime slumbers and daily afternoon naps. His countless hours in repose became the means of an endless nightmare. The gypsy assured me that upon my death, the noose would haunt Rodrigo's sleep until death overtook him. Even while awake, Rodrigo would feel the hangman's knot behind his right ear, slowly tightening and choking off his air supply. Rodrigo's invisible hangman followed behind, shadowing every waking moment.

In a desperate attempt to stop the ghastly dreams and waking dread, Rodrigo hanged himself. His dust and bones are not far beyond the very tree that shades my tomb. I commend the gypsy for that fine revenge. I cannot recall how often I have attempted to tell this tale, but until your visit, none had been courteous enough to stop and listen."

A shadow crossed the gravestone and briefly, the face of Armond appeared.

"Depart now young sir. Look not to your own for answers in this place. Know well one thing; not all written accounts of heroes are true. Learn from what you have heard here today. Greed, betrayal, and disloyalty are among the foulest of sins. They bare a terrible price and those who succumb to their treaty are damned. Continue on your journey with care, but do not look to a hero's nest, for it is long depleted."

Relieved by the parting words, the young soldier removed his cap and gloves and brushing away the leaves and weeds from the headstone, he paused in steely silence in reverence of the long dead, but well deserved spirit. He then stood upright at attention and saluted. With tempered resolve and a tear in his eye, the young man departed to continue the search for his namesake, a man named Rodrigo Santiago. Shortly thereafter he stumbled onto Rodrigo's grave and he paused briefly to observe the headstone's inscription. "Here lies Rodrigo, the patriot. May his deeds live on in history," and as he traced the words cut into stone, neither reverence nor adoration showed on his face. Turning away, he voiced, "This story must be repealed," a confirmation of the silent vow made at the grave of Armond Balosteros.

THE END

Meow !

It was nearly three o'clock on a Monday morning and mid-town Manhattan was quiet for a change. As he drove down a deserted street near his condo, Harvey Noonan reached for a ringing cell phone.

"Yeah, this is Harvey." A long silence followed. "Why are you calling me with this trivial BS ... don't you know it's three o'clock in the morning?" He listened intently for a moment but quickly turned on the caller, "Well, I don't give a crap about that. You're not coming back to stay with me ... just because ... " His mouth stretched and he scrunched up his nose, making a monkey face.

"You've been screwing around with me for too long and I'm not going to take you back." The young woman on the other end of the line began to plead,

"But I've nowhere to go, Harvey, please ... at least let me stay with you for a couple of nights. I'll even sleep on the sofa. I won't be a bother." Harvey relaxed, thinking that it would be nice to have the condo cleaned.

"OK then, if you are willing to clean up the condo for me, I'll let you stay, but just for a few nights."

"Oh Harvey, I'll do more than that if you want," she cooed.

"No, I don't want anything like that. I've sworn off sex for awhile ... got to get my head straight." Secretly, Harvey wished for a toss in the bed with Gretchen. She was a great lay and as he turned from the main street comer, he could feel his manhood swelling at the prospect. But then he'd be trapped again just like the last time he took her back. "Let's play this one straight. I can't afford to get involved right now."

"OK Harvey," she answered, "but all you have to do is ask and I'm game." "Fine," he said, "I'll call ahead to night shift security and have them let you into my place." He hung up.

Noonan dialed the condo security office with the approval for Gretchen to receive a key to the apartment. With the phone plastered to his ear and one hand on the wheel, he didn't notice the shadow emerge from a side street alley. Suddenly, a black mass shot out from behind the backlit shadow. With a screech, Harvey's Toyota came to a sliding halt, but not before experiencing a thump under one of its tires.

"Jesus!" he exclaimed and he looked in the car's rear view mirror. Behind him an eight pound lump of black fur lay in the middle of a moonlit street. "Oh crap, you did it now," he exclaimed. Unbuckling his seatbelt, Harvey sat for a few moments gazing at the mirror. The ball of fur did not move so he re-buckled, but as he was about to take off, Noonan glanced one more time. A shiver went up his spine as he detected slight movement of one paw. "It's a cat! Oh crap, it's still alive." A rush of adrenaline overtook him and coupled by a morbid curiosity, Harvey again released the seatbelt buckle. Stepping out of the car, he walked over to the flattened mass of fur and bone. As he approached he could see that the cat was solid black. Its paws were twitching. Must be an uncontrollable spasm, he thought. Cat 's probably dead and this is just a reflex action.

The street was deserted and a light rain began to fall. Flipping up his jacket collar, Harvey decided to look for something to use to move the cat. He didn't dare pick it up in his hands for fear of blood or guts that might slip out from among the fur. "Yuck," he groused as he picked up a moist brown bag laying in the gutter. Placing it next to the cat, he gently rolled the carcass over. As it came to rest on the bag, the cat's eyes opened slightly. "Holly crap, he's alive!"

Harvey was more scared than glad to see that the cat had survived, but it was certain to die from its injuries. He picked up the makeshift litter and carried the injured feline over to his car. Opening the trunk, Harvey placed the dying cat in the opening. Got to get it to a vet, he thought. But then the reality hit him. It was the middle of the night and there would be no animal clinics open to receive the victim of his Toyota. As he closed the trunk Noonan heard a whimper. The cat's eyes opened, glowing red in the moonlight. It cried out as if to say, don't leave me. "Oh geez, I'm gonna have bad luck now." He remembered the old saying- never cross directly in the path of a black cat. "That's just what I need," he muttered, thinking of Gretchen tooling around in his apartment. "She's probably drinking all my booze and stealing me blind while

I'm out here trying to take care of this old cat."

Throwing down the trunk lid, Harvey wiped off the residue from the bag onto his jacket. "Yuck, now I smell like wet newspaper." Fumbling with his keys, he jumped back into the car and took off. Ten minutes later he was at the condo's underground parking lot. Finding his reserved space, Harvey pulled in and shut down the engine. "OK, now what?" he fumed. The cat was still in the trunk and he hoped that when he opened it, he'd find it dead. "Oh, crap, what if he 's still alive? "

The parking lot security guard, an old black man dressed in uniform sat near the building's central elevator shaft. Waking up from the noise of Harvey's Toyota, he stretched his arms above his head, and then waived a hello. Harvey returned it. An instant later, he called the man over to the car. "Jeremiah, come over here and help me with something." He pulled up the trunk lid bent over while waiving the man over to the car.

"What's you got there Mr. Noonan?" As he reached the car, he peered over Harvey's shoulder. "Oh, a dead cat ... what-chu-do, Mr. Noonan, run over it?"

"Yeah, about ten blocks back. He was still alive when I put him in ... looks dead now, doesn't he?" The old man took a closer look, backed away and shrugged. "Don't know but that's a black cat, Mr. Noonan. Bad luck comes to those who cross paths with the black cat."

"I know the old wives tale. Can you help me discard this thing?"

"No sir, I isn't touching no dead black cat. There's them that says that the bad luck follows any who gets involved. The bad is on you now Mr. Noonan. I don't want no part of it ... sorry sir."

Harvey pulled a wad of money from his pocket. "How's about one hundred dollars to get rid of it." The security guard's eyes widened.

"A hundred? Well sir, how's about I supply the trash can and walks it out to the curb. You gotta pull it out and put it in the can, and then I'll walk it out to the curb for a hundred. "

"OK, you got a deal." Harvey turned back to the trunk and pulled on the sides of the bag. As he began to lift the cat out of the trunk it screeched out in pain. "Yeooow!"
Harvey dropped the bag and looked over to the security guard. "The cat's still alive… now what?"

The old man had been moving a plastic trash can from the guard shack and stopped in his tracks. "No deal, you can keep the money." He shook his head sternly. "Mr. Noonan, that cat's still got lives left in him. You can't just throw him away now. You'd better take him up to your apartment and doctor him 'till morning. I'll see to it that the animal clinic sends someone over as soon as they open."

Harvey pleaded but to no avail. "All right then, but can you get me something soft but strong enough to hold him so I can take him upstairs?"

"How's about a cardboard box?" the old man replied, "Got one in the shack." He turned and slid back to his duty station. Moments later he came back with a banana crate stuffed with a folded up towel. "Might as well make him comfortable, Mr. Noonan."

Harvey nodded, "Yeah, well here." He handed the guard the one hundred dollar bill.

"This is for your trouble."

"Thank you sir, it's been a pleasure helping such a fine

young man." The guard looked into the back of the car.

"Oh Jesus, that's one of them devil cats, sir. They got them red eyes. That means they gots a black heart. Can't trust them devil cats sir. You should take him away from here or something bad'll happen for sure."

Perturbed, Noonan grabbed the box. "Go tend to your shack, old man. I'm gonna do this myself."

"Ok sir, I'm just say' in ... " His voice trailed off. Skulking back to his chair, he added, "But I do appreciate the money." Pulling up a copy of Ebony magazine, the old guard turned away from Noonan. Opening the cover he remarked again shaking his head, "Can't trust those devil cats, no sir."

As Noonan reached the apartment with his box in hand, the cat still cradled in the bag, he pulled out the condo keys. Suddenly the door opened. "Hi sweetie!" It was Gretchen. "Oh what you got there?" She looked at the mass of fur and bloodstains. "Oh Harvey, what happened?"

"It's a long story ... ran over this cat about ten blocks away. It's not dead yet and the guard downstairs won't take it off my hands. I'm gonna keep it here until morning and then the animal shelter will come and get him."

"What'll they do with him?" She seemed more concerned for the feline than for its handler.

"Probably euthanize it I suppose," Harvey said shrugging his shoulders.

"Oh poor thing," she stroked the slightly wet fur and from somewhere within, the cat began purring. "Maybe he's not too hurt?"

"Look," Harvey pleaded, "can't we just forget this now. I'm

tired and I want to go to bed."

"Oh Harvey, so you changed your mind?"

"No, I want to go to bed, not have sex."

"OK then," Gretchen pushed back verbally, "you don't have to be so mean about it. Let me take the cat into the kitchen. I'll clean him up as best I can; make him comfortable. You go take a shower and leave it to me."

Harvey liked that idea. "Fine, tend to the cat. I'll be out in a few, and then we'll talk."

Noonan walked away leaving Gretchen pulling at the paper bag beneath the cat's body. It was bloody and wet and when she'd finished, the cat rolled over on his other side. She gently wiped him down taking note of his injuries. His back legs and tail were mangled but his upper body looked normal except for matted blood near his shoulder. "I think you may make it, young man," she whispered. The cat purred ever so slightly and blinked. "Yes, you understand don't you?" Gretchen fondled his ears lovingly.

Fifteen minutes later, Harvey emerged from the bathroom. "Are you OK in there?" he called out. There was no answer. "Gretchen?" Harvey walked through the swinging door to the kitchen. "Gretchen?" She was sitting at the table draped over the box. "Gretchen?" There was no movement. She must have fallen asleep, he thought. Gently from behind he touched her shoulder. "Gretchen, wake up." She did not move. Nervously, Harvey began rocking her shoulder back and forth; still no movement. In the box, the injured cat opened its eyes. "Meoooow." The sudden sound shook Noonan and he made his way around to the side of the table. Getting a closer look at Gretchen, he saw the blood matted in her hair. Lifting her head, Harvey gasped. Both of Gretchen's eyes had been gouged out; bite and deep flesh wounds covered her face. The trauma of seeing her condition caused him to double over and puke. Then he noticed the cat's front paws, nails extended and bloody.

"You did this?" he questioned. The cat looked up at him, its eyes showing evil intent. It screeched, throwing out its front appendages. Harvey stepped back in horror. "Little bastard, you're gonna pay for this." He picked up a kitchen knife from its caddy on the counter. Turning back to the cat he held it high over his head. "I'm gonna finish this right now," he growled. Moving forward, Harvey's face contorted. Without warning Gretchen lifted her head, her eye sockets a mixture of blood and tissue. She grabbed his free arm and stopped him from lunging at his adversary. "Meoooow!" As if on orders from the cat, Gretchen stood up and with her back to the feline, faced Harvey.

"Oh Gretchen, what has it done to you?" She smiled and as words poured out, Harvey thought, this is not Gretchen speaking.

"No Harvey, you cannot kill me. You tried but could not with your car. What makes you think you can do it now?" Noonan dropped the knife and held onto Gretchen with both hands. "I've got to get you to the hospital. C'mon Gretch, let's go. I'll take care of that cat later." He looked over to the cat, now perched up on its front legs. Its eyes blazed blood red and Harvey noticed his tongue flicking in and out. Gretchen lowered her bloody head and slumped into his arms. As Noonan dragged her dead body weight into the living room, he called back, "I'm coming back for you, you little bastard ... hear me? I'm coming back to finish you off."

Harvey sat Gretchen's near lifeless body down on the sofa and she slumped over on a throw pillow. Picking up the house phone he called down to the security guard at the front desk. "Hello, Pete, I need an ambulance right quick. Have one sent to the building ASAP."

"What's the emergency, Mr. Noonan?"

"Just call them now," he shouted through the phone. Pulling himself together, Harvey shuffled into the bathroom and pulled some hand towels from the linen closet. Dousing them in water, he hustled back to the living room and tried his best to clean up the open wounds on Gretchen's face. Still passed out on the sofa, the young victim began to twitch as the compress passed over her bloody face. "Meoooow!" From the kitchen, the plaintive sounds of a cat in pain echoed within the apartment.

"Damned cat, shut up will you?" he groused. Pulling up from the sofa, Harvey snuck a look into the kitchen. Passing through the door, he peered into the box on the table. "Meoooow!"

"Little bastard, you're going back to hell, right where you came from."

As he finished his sentence, Harvey heard a strange gurgle coming from the cat. It began to spasm and regurgitate. With a series of twitches the black cat threw up a large hairball of Gretchen's blonde main. Again it began to spasm and another hairball coughed up into the box. Harvey watched as three more times the cat puked up blonde hairballs. As the last one settled onto the makeshift bed, the first began to grow. As it puffed up, Harvey could see that it began to take the shape of a cat, blonde and furry as if regenerating from a hairy seedpod. The second, then the third began to stir and in a few moments all five of the hairballs began regenerating into blonde cats in the box.

"Holy shit," Harvey exclaimed, "how the hell did you do that?"

The black cat sat up. Its rear still incapacitated, dragged behind, the flattened tail involuntarily flopping around at the end. Noonan caught a glimpse of a sly smile as it watched the unearthly clones generate into living felines. Once all were fully formed they cuddled about their master. Following several subtle blinks of an eye he called out instructions to them. "Meooooow!"

Harvey Noonan now stood immobile and in awe of the devil cat and its five feline clones. "Meoooow," it repeated again and again as on cue each attacked the hapless victim.

* * *

There was a sharp knock at the door to Harvey Noonan's apartment. After several attempts, the sound of a whimpering cat came from within.

"What do we do now?" the first paramedic asked. The morning shift security guard blurted out from behind them,

"I can't unlock the door without permission unless you guys are willing to take responsibility."

"The paramedic took charge. "Listen Bob or Joe, or whatever your name is, the night shift guard is the one who called. You're in charge now."

"I suppose, but Mr. Noonan didn't talk to me so I'm not gonna open the door unless you two order me to do it."

The lead paramedic shook his head. "Yeah, I know, these days nobody wants to take responsibility for anything, even if someone is dying. There is probable cause since Noonan made the call. I'm sure that's posted in the security log, so just do it … 1'11 take responsibility. "

"OK man, you're the boss, and the name is Virgil." he quipped. Breaking out the master keys, he unlocked the door. They entered and immediately noticed Gretchen lying on the sofa. "Oh geez-us!" the lead paramedic exclaimed. Three furry blonde cats looked up from the lap of her lifeless body. "Oh my God!" the security guard exclaimed. Moving quickly, the paramedics went to work moving the little critters and checking her vitals.

"She's expired," one said. "Let's double check the other countered and they lay her down to look for the first signs of rigor. "Yep, see the blue line across her lower abdomen?"

"Geez, what happened here?" the other asked. They rearranged the body securely on the sofa while the guard called in to the police department. "Looks like domestic trouble," the guard called out on his phone." He turned to the paramedics. "Somebody took it out on that poor young girl." As they managed the scene the security guard moved into the bedroom and adjoining bath area. Feeling the need, he closed the bathroom door and quickly relieved himself.

Finished with the sudden call to nature he called out, "Nothing here. I'll check the kitchen." The toilet flushed and he moved onto the kitchen.

Entered through the kitchen door, the guard gasped. "Here, come quick," he shouted. The lead medic bolted through the doorway. "Oh my God, what the hell .... " His words trailed off to a whisper as he tried to make sense of the scene. On the kitchen table, a black cat lay in its makeshift cardboard bed. Nearby on the floor lay the body of Harvey Noonan. His face puffed up, a swollen tongue protruding from between purple lips. It was easy to see that Harvey Noonan was deceased. Two cats lay purring on his chest.

When the men approached the cats shrieked, hissing loudly. They sat up and struck out menacingly as the paramedic began to check Harvey for signs of life. In the box, the black cat responded, "Meoooow," and immediately they settled down.

"Little buggers don't know that their master is dead."

"Trying to protect him I guess," the security guard said.

"Ok, nothing we can do here. Let's call it in." The paramedic slipped over two the older black cat. "Poor guy,...looks like you've been squished by a car." He called over to the dispatch on his mobile phone,

"Let's get animal control over to the West Avenue Apartments, number 22-B. We've got a large male cat that needs vet care ... oh yeah, and five smaller cats that need to be placed in a shelter."

Still on the mobile phone he turned back to the dead man on the kitchen floor.

"I don't know what happened here ... No, looks like a murder-suicide to me." He waited for a response. Moments later he answered, "No, looks like the guy tore up his girlfriend, then went into the kitchen and sliced his throat open. There's blood all over the place." Again he waited for a response.

"No, I don't know about the cats...1ittle devils are a strange brood. Found them perched on the bodies pruning the blood from their paws and mouths. Never seen anything like it before ... no, cats lapping up human blood." He waited for a response and with his last transmission all he could say was, "Go figure."

As he was leaving the kitchen an animal control technician knocked on the condo's door. Opening it, the guard hustled her into the apartment.

"Someone called about a cat needing vet services?" She looked at the body of Gretchen and nearly fainted. "Oh lord, what happened?"

"Never mind," the senior paramedic said, "there are six cats in all. The one in the kitchen is injured."
The vet assistant stammered,

"I ... we had a ... a voicemail that there was a large cat to be picked up. Now you say there are six?" Hands on her hips, she postured,

"I'm not prepared to take six cats." As she finished, the five blonde cats scampered passed them bolting out the open apartment door.

"Oh great, now I've got five strays to catch." She turned and chased down the hallway after them. Inside, the injured black cat cried out, "Meoooow!"

THE END

THIRST

Never before had it felt
A chill deep to the marrow
But the beggar's throat beckoned.
The blood, vile, cold and salty
Seemed devoid of sustenance
Like none other experienced.
It longed for fresh victims
Well beyond the foggy-bottom
And dank harbor warehouses.
It sought only to feed again
But not on depleted lifeblood
Of disease-ridden hosts.
When the sullen predator
Purged the last tainted drops
It was time to carry on.
The immortal moved uptown
Where the upper class dined
On goose liver and lamb.
There he watched intently
As young sweet maidens
Primped and readied for bed.
Soon they would sleep
Then it would take its fill
From those well-healed cups.

E.W. Bonadio

Incarnation

The airborne attack was swift and sudden. Twenty-two members of the Islamic terrorist group had been killed by strategically placed cruise missiles fired from a missile frigate stationed in the Arabian Gulf. Those that survived the early morning onslaught managed to slip away from the ruined camp. Now, all that remained was the aftermath of death and destruction. For Major Jonah Diggs, the insertion of his Ranger team was the only thing left to accomplish. He was there to clean up, document the kills, collect intelligence and then supervise the extraction of his team back to the U.N. camp.

"Not long now Nazir," he yelled over the roar of the chopper's turbine driven blades. Looking down at his wristwatch, Diggs continued, "Just a few clicks to the west."

Holding onto his loosely fitting helmet, the Egyptian shifted uneasily in his seat. He nodded briefly and grabbed onto a handhold just above his shoulder. Just then the helicopter pitched to the left then banked right cresting the hilly terrain into the valley below. It was a basic evasive maneuver to counter an ambush of RPG's or small arms fire. The Egyptian officer knew that if they were to encounter hostiles it would be as they descended into the valley. Nazir released his grip and pointed with his free hand to the remains of the camp. "There it is Major, just in front of us now." Rich plums of black smoke rose from the smoldering ruins, distinctly marking their objective. As the choppers approached the landing zone, Diggs could see the main camp structure, a mud brick building, ringed by several tents and a few vehicles. Nearby, a stand of indigenous trees stood among tall grasses and an ancient watering hole, the lifeblood of the camp.

"Here we go," Diggs yelled, "lock and load." Nazir smiled thinly, shaking his head at the bravado emanating from his counterpart.

The two U.N. designated helicopters swooped down and landed on the desert floor between two ridges. Diggs's small force was in Egypt, just a few miles from an ancient ruin near the western bank of the Nile River. The major's mission objective was politically sensitive, and he was thankful for the Egyptian government's help and the five Arab soldiers under the command of Nazir el Ghazi.

"OK, everybody out," Diggs commanded from his jump seat. Nazir's men were the first to clear the landing zone. Under orders, they trekked over to the roofless one story hut where many of the terrorist bodies lay. As the helicopters ascended turning away from the camp, Diggs' immediate task was to secure the camp and he went about it coolly, placing men at strategic fire points. After a thorough search of the camp, the Egyptian found Diggs rummaging through a semi-collapsed storage tent. Nazir strolled into the tent and the major could see in his eyes that the main objective was lost.

"Sorry to say that there are none left alive, major. They must have took the wounded and left only the dead. My men are gathering the bodies now for identification and disposal."

"Too bad," Diggs countered, "I was hoping to catch one still alive. We need INTEL." Leaving the Egyptian's side and sliding out of the tent, major Diggs looked around for his ranger squad leader. Finding him taking a smoke break with an Egyptian soldier he barked, "Sergeant Pennington, get two men to search the area near that vehicle." He pointed to a partially wrecked red Toyota truck sitting a few yards from the camp's ancient cistern. With a quick salute, Pennington dropped the smoke crushing it with his boot heel, calling out as he jogged away, " Smith... Gordon, come with me." Arriving at the truck, Pennington rummaged through the cab. The others rooted around the ancient watering hole flipping over sheets of metal and examining barrels and boxes strewn around the area.

Minutes later, Pennington returned to Diggs carrying a satchel under his arm. "Gordon retrieved this from a spot near the well, sir... Bet one of the jihadists dropped it while booking from the camp." Diggs grabbed the bag and investigated. Opening the flap he peered in, then dug deep into the canvas pouch. "Shit son, all you brought me was stone tablet...some pictures on it. What is this stuff?" Pennington shrugged. Looking back to the Egyptian officer, Diggs bellowed, "Nazir, come over here will you." As he approached, Diggs threw the heavy package over to him. "Got any ideas what this is?"

Temporarily caught off guard, Nazir blinked. Quickly, he brushed a thin layer of sand and dirt from his face. Opening the satchel, the Egyptian pulled out the tablet. "It's Hieroglyphics, major, ancient Egyptian writings etched into stone."

"Well, what do you suppose the terrorists want with it?" Diggs queried.
Nazir shook his head slowly. Then a thought came to him. "Mohammad, come over here," he shouted in Arabic. A young Egyptian soldier helping with the collection of the dead dropped his end of a badly burned body and raced over to his superior. With

a sharp salute, he clicked his heals saying, "Reporting as ordered, sir."

"Mohammad, what do you make of this?" The young man took the satchel and pulled out the stone tablet. He shook off the dirt and sand covering the inscriptions and studied the pictures. "Oh Allah be merciful," he declared, "It's the spell of regeneration." Nazir shook his head. "You meant the book of the dead."

Mohammad did not want to counter his superior, but he knew that Nazir was mistaken. "No sir, not quite. This is a banned spell, purportedly used by a high priest who rebelled against the Pharaoh Ankhenaten. It was supposedly a gift from the God Anubis, created to raise a personal army of the dead. But the priest was executed before an army could be raised to challenge Pharaoh. That was over three thousand years ago. Only the myth of that priest ever existed. That is until now."

"That doesn't make any sense," Diggs said. "How'd you know...could you really read this stuff?"
Mohammad smiled shyly, "Yes sir, I was a university student, but I got called into the Army last June. My specialty in school was ancient Egyptian mythology and writings."

Nazir bit down hard on his lip. "Major, I have heard of a cult in this region of Egypt. It's headed by an IMAM who wants to bring back the dead to help fight off the invasion by Westerners. It could be that..."

Diggs stopped Nazir in mid sentence. "Now hold on Captain. You mean to tell me that they were trying to raise the dead to fight us?" Nazir's lips pursed as he tried to come up with an intelligent answer. "Well Diggs I must confide, when the tablet was being translated I heard a faint groan coming from over there." He pointed to the well. "It was as if one of the dead had begun to come back to life. But the noise stopped."

"That's ridicules," the major challenged, "But I'll give you this, those dead corpses over there would certainly like to be the first ones reincarnated." He pointed to the mud brick structure where nearly two dozen dead terrorists lay.

Nazir was not laughing. "I tell you major, if the spell of the ancients is spoken properly and the power of the one that controls this spell is strong, there are some that believe they might rise to fight again."

"Is that so?" Diggs grabbed the stone from Mohammad. Laughing out loud, the major said, "Let's test that theory." He studied the tablet for a moment, then gave it back to the Egyptian soldier. "All right son, just read it out for us just as it is written" The young Egyptian looked over to his leader. Nazir reluctantly nodded his approval and Mohammad began to translate in Egyptian. After a few words, Diggs stopped him. "No son, in English...say it in English. I want to understand the words."

"By the light of RA and the staff of Anubis, I call upon the gods of our forefathers. My brother, rise up to live and fight again." Mohammad fell silent and then suddenly, as if in a trance, he began to collapse. The Egyptian captain held him by the shoulders, keeping the boy from collapsing. Mohammad had properly chanted the spell of awakening and it had nearly consumed him. Shaken by the experience, Nazir protested, "I want my people out of here by nightfall. You may stay if you wish, but I would not trust this place now that we have dishonored the past and our ancestors."

Major Diggs laughed. "So you are afraid of a little ancient hocus pocus are you? Ok, I'll have your men extracted within the hour. My team is staying tonight. We'll show you that your ancient rites don't scare American rangers. Besides, we have to RECON the area and finish the mission."

Two hours later, Nazir and his team were on a chopper heading back to the U.N. base camp. The Egyptian took the stone with him, promising Mohammad, "You are not to blame for the words you spoke, but I fear that we have inadvertently awakened a terrible thing, an evil hidden for centuries. The stone will go back to the authorities. I will make a report and see to it that the tablet reaches the museum of antiquities in Cairo."

Mohammad agreed, "There is no other choice but to place it into the hands of our learned men. I am glad that we have retrieved such an important artifact." Mohammad accepted the task of protecting the tablet on their trip back to base. But the young soldier refused to unwrap the stone to show it off or explain the dread that came over him as he read the spell. He vowed never to speak the words again in any language.

Fearing the terrorists' return, Diggs re-set the perimeter around the camp. The bodies of the dead Islamists lay stretched out in front of the burned out hut. Five of the rangers had bunked inside the hut. Two sentries secured the eastern perimeter and similar pairs lay north and west of the hut. Major Diggs took up residence in the bed of the Toyota truck at the southern edge of compound.

At midnight, the carnage began. One by one, the terrorist bodies came to life and they lay in front of the building waiting for the command to take action. When fully reincarnated the terrorists received orders and they fell on the unsuspecting rangers in the hut. No shots rang out, but the muffled death throws of the rangers in the burned out hut alerted the sentries on duty. As they stared out through night vision goggles they had no idea of the threat from behind. Unseen attackers wielding rocks, shovels and other makeshift weapons dispatched the sentries until only Pennington remained on the perimeter.

Diggs and Pennington were still alive. The major lay sleeping in the back of the Toyota. Pennington had taken temporarily residence in a tent halfway between the truck and the hut. Dead silence filled the air around camp and as Pennington roused to relieve himself they came at him. Leaving the tent, he noticed three reincarnated terrorists. Holding a bayonet within striking distance, the lead one struck. In the Toyota, something stirred within Diggs, rousing him from sleep. The feeling of certain doom channeled by Nazir's fears and his own bad dreams forced Diggs awake. Lines of sweat poured down his brow and his eyes opened just in time to hear the muffled screams coming from the tent. Something was terribly wrong and instinctively, Diggs bristled. He dared not call out for fear of giving away his position so quietly, he pulled out his combat phone. Diggs pressed the call button. "Gordon...Pennington... anybody there?"

The last living Ranger released the button and waited. Suddenly, something caught his attention as strange sounds began to sift through the air. Crawling out from the darkness of that ancient pit, the reconstructing body of the priest pressed on to complete his own mission. Echoes of falling debris with occasional splatters of mud plunking into the water drew his attention and Diggs sat up. The entity was alive, ascending from his watery grave. The evil entity had festered in his dark prison for centuries and his incarnate soul longed for a day of reckoning. Thrown into the cistern by Pharaoh's soldiers, he had long ago decayed until nothing was left but minute particles of dust and DNA. It was an unfitting end to his human form, a body that could be reconstituted only by the properly spoken recitation of the spell. Pharaoh's soldiers had foolishly thrown the tablet down the well along with his broken body. How stupid, he thought, to have left the means of my regeneration so close. All the evil entity needed was someone to retrieve the stone and speak the words of regeneration. By the time he reached the lip of the well his human form had only partially reconstituted. Now he needed a donor, someone whose life essence could bring the body completely back to its original form, this time as the immortal champion of dead souls.

In the truck, Diggs locked and loaded his trusty 45 automatic. It had served him well in previous actions and he knew how to use it. Reaching over the side of the truck bed and gently lifting his head above the rail, Diggs looked for signs of life. Through night vision goggles he spied shadowy forms moving forward toward the Toyota. Peering over to the hut, he saw the bodies of his rangers, now devoid of life. The regenerated attackers had laid them to rest in the same spot where they were displayed that afternoon. Diggs threw off his night vision goggles and squinted and his eyes adjusted to the darkness. He could make out their faces better as the undead closed in on his position. Each of the walking re-animated killing machines had but one purpose now, capturing Diggs so that his life form could be used to help fully restore their new master.

"Goddamn zombie bastards," he shouted. Instinctively, the pistol fired - bam, bam, bam...one by one they dropped in a heap. When the magazine emptied, Diggs drew another clip and quickly shoved it into the butt. Again, shots rang out in rapid-fire succession. The zombie attackers continued their methodical assault against Diggs's well-placed fire until the last of them hit the ground, dead for the second time that day.

Drained by the experience, the major fell back into the Toyota's bed. Diggs mind raced uncontrollably. He tried desperately to understand what had happened. Fearing for his life Diggs rolled over onto his belly and grabbed for his field phone. Whispering into it, he said, "May-day, may-day, come in GREEN DRAGON 4, this is BRAVO DELTA 6, over?" There was no answer. After a short silence, he called out forcefully, "GREEN DRAGON 4, this is BRAVO DELTA 4, we have casualties and need assistance. Request a transport and support, over?" This time they answered. "Negative, no can do, sir. You'll have to hold out 'till 0-700 hours." It was nighttime in the Egyptian desert and help would not come until morning.

Diggs sat up in the bed of the truck and listened for sounds of activity. Instinctively, he felt an evil presence in the darkness near the ancient well. He pointed his pistol, ready to shoot at anything that moved, but the blackness of the night left him unsure of whom, or what was still out there. It could be one of my men, he thought. Diggs hoped desperately that he was not alone, that another ranger had survived the zombie attack. "Hey out there...Bravo team...is that you?" A low grunt, followed by a wisp of shadowy movement made Diggs realize that something was heading in his direction.

"Hello, Bravo team, report or be shot," he challenged. Still, there was no answer, just the sound shuffling forward in the desert night. Sweat poured down his cheeks as Diggs drew a bead in the general direction of the noise. Then he moved it off-center and fired two rounds. POW – POW!

The ploy did not work and the phantom intruder edged closer to the truck. Fear gripped at Diggs and he hyperventilated close to the point of blacking out. Catching his breath, he dropped down into the truck's bed and fumbled nervously with his ranger flashlight. Pulling it free from the webbing, he pressed on the rubberized switch – nothing. "Goddamnit!" he exclaimed. Banging it twice on the rail, he clicked again and the light flickered on. His next move was both daring and tactical. With his 45 automatic in his left hand and the illuminated flashlight in his right, Diggs pulled himself up over the truck's railing. Again, he flicked it on.

The beam from the flashlight focused on a grotesque form, that of the mummy priest and Major Diggs screamed. The sound reverberated among the ridges ringing the camp. Nazir was correct. They had unleashed an evil on the world, one that was bent on using Diggs as its host. It was a hideous monster, a demon from that ancient well of time reeking of pure hate and malice. For over three thousand years the creature waited patiently for its freedom. Now, because of a chance encounter between a few misguided Islamists and the unsuspecting foreign infidels, it was back among the living, back to seek revenge.

Now partially restored by the words of Mohammad, the mummy was still regenerating. But he needed fresh blood and life fluids that only the living possessed. Confronting Major Diggs at the truck, it regarded the unbeliever. It could sense his life force. It was strong in the Major and the priest was glad to have spared him. Diggs would be the mummy's first sacrifice. The priest would require others to keep his newly regenerated body viable and as with Diggs, he would choose them well. The terrorist leaders had been useful servants. They would continue to be of use to him. Digging up the tablet in an attempt to use it for their evil purposes had been foolhardy. They possessed no such power. The prophecies and stories of the tablet of regeneration were certainly true, but not as the terrorist leaders had hoped. The priest's banishment to the underworld had been useful as well and his malice grew with each passing year. The hate inside drove him to what he was about to do. The terrorists killed by the infidels had provided the muscle needed to rid the camp of the intruders. Now only Major Diggs remained, and the mummy meant to make quick work of him.

The next morning two Army helicopters arrived, bringing in twenty-six additional soldiers from the U.N. base camp near Cairo. They found nothing but death and destruction. During the search the soldiers found Major Diggs sitting up in the bed of the truck, his lifeless eyes set deep into hollow sockets. The Major's desiccated body barely filled out his once proud uniform. The essence of his body was gone, replaced by a shallow shell of clothes, bone and skin. The officer in charge of the rescue reported to base, "We found Major Diggs. He looks like a three thousand year old mummy." No other sign of life remained in the ruins of the terrorist camp.

Miles from the camp the completely regenerated form of the priest rested at an outcropping overlooking the Nile River. The hard work of re-incarnation was now behind him.
Wearing traditional Egyptian garb taken from a Bedouin sheepherder, he watched as small sailboats navigated the river. The stone tablet of regeneration was safe in Cairo, hidden away in a museum vault. The incarnate needed to finish what had been started nearly three thousand years before when the world of man was young. He yearned to understand and learn from the advances made in weaponry and other tools of war. Only then would his power be complete.

Within the week the priest arrived in the ancient capital city. Assuming the form of an Egyptian scholar, one selected from a list of Egyptologists currently on the museum staff, he readied himself for the task. Strolling up the steps of the museum building the incarnate had come to reclaim his army. With the tablet safely in his hands he expected nothing less than dominion over the graven fools who tried so ineptly to use its power.

THE END

THE DINER

Dark shadows spilled over the roadway as the trio made their way north to Bailey's Corner. The midnight hour had long since passed and those who still chose to be out did so at their peril. The undead had come to feed and there was not much the people of the small sleepy Appalachian town could do to stop them. The local authorities had been warned. Stories of the strange series of murders in Sidwell, just six miles down the road from Bailey's Corner had made it to town. The voice message, followed by a fax from Sidwell's sheriff cautioned that the killers were on their way. It was a matter for law enforcement professionals but that tactic had failed so many times before.

Sheriff Joe Krebbs laughed at the report. Tossing it over to the young officer sitting at his desk, he quipped "So we've got some hoodlum devil-worshipers on the loose. I've encountered toughs like these before and I'll betcha they'll yelp like dogs when I open up on 'em." As he read the fax, the deputy shook his head. "Seven dead in just four days ... says here that they'd been drained of blood. Damn!"

"Now don't go getting all bunched up, Jimmy." Krebbs pulled out his service revolver, a silvered 44 magnum with a six-inch barrel.

Fingering the trigger, he got into the shooter's stance. "I'll blow those mother-effers away right quick with this here cannon."

"Seven dead, Sheriff," the young man repeated, "and we don't even have mug shots or rap sheets on 'em. How you suppose we will know 'em when they come?"

Getting up to replenish his coffee the young man continued, "The fax says that there are three of 'em, two guys and a young girl." He paced the room waiting for the next cup of java to flow from the single cup coffee brewer. "Sheriff Bramford reports that he shot one of them twice in the torso and they didn't go down." Krebbs nodded slightly replying,

"His voicemail said that the perp just walked away from one of the victims and never even looked back. Guess he didn't want to risk a head-shot by confronting the law."

"That's spooky, sir. It sounds like something out of a horror comic book. "

"Yeah, I don't know about that stuff...above my pay grade and all. I'm no detective but I got a hunch. They must be wearing body armor. No problem, my forty-four will knock 'em down even if those perps are wearing the newest Kevlar. This here gun's a powerful piece." He stroked the side of his sidearm.

"No guns," the deputy countered, "why wear body armor without a gun to shoot it out with against the law? This is a strange bunch sheriff."

"Yeah, they must be some fanatical splinter of a satanic cult." The deputy took a sip of his coffee and sat back down. "The report says they must've used knives to slit the throats of their victims ... then they licked the blood as it poured out."

"Damnation, son, I don't know about that." Sheriff Krebs growled, "but they'll be coming up along the Gunpowder River road. Bramford's fax says they are probably on foot so they'll be to edge of town soon." The deputy shook his head. "Why didn't the Sidwell police try to follow and arrest them?" Krebbs looked down at his digital watch. "Don't know, maybe their scared of getting slit throats. No time to worry about that. .. let's get rollin."

The Bailey's all-night diner sat at the edge of town. Inside, Tanner, the recently hired cook sat at the doorway to the kitchen. It was nearly two in the morning and with no orders to fill, he thumbed through a Captain America comic book retrieved from the men's room. Night-shift waitress, Kirby Smith strolled through the diner serving the remaining customers refills of coffee. As she made her way to the booth near the diner's front door Kirby was greeted with a hand in her face.

"Geez Kirby, can't you see...I got plenty left here in my cup." Billy Lourdes snapped open his twenty year old Zippo lighter and lit up a smoke. "Got this from my dad just before he died. Just about the only thing of value he had to his name." He lit up a Marlborough red and took a long drag. Peering outside, he remarked, "Oh no, here comes trouble."

A late night visitor to the diner arrived, this one not unknown to the people inside. Wearing a black leather jacket with the insignia Hell's Angels Motorcycle Club and sporting a tricked out Harley

Fat-Boy, this customer was more than just a regular. Pushing through the double glass doors, he breezed past the waitress, but not before patting her roughly on the butt.

"Hey, watch it buster," she commanded. Smiling broadly, he made his way to the lunch counter and parked on a stool. From behind Kirby gave him the single digit salute.

"Ass hole." She then turned back to the young man in the booth.

"Can't do that in here anymore, Billy." Kirby pulled out the smoke from between his lips and dowsed the cigarette in his water glass.

"Shit girl, don't you know how much these things cost? Now you get no tip."

"Wasn't expecting much anyway, Billy … you've always been a bad tipper."

Over at the counter, the motorcycle man snapped up a nearby empty coffee mug and spoon. Clanking it against the side of cup he turned to the waitress. "How's about some coffee over here, sweetie." Kirby shot him a look.

"Hold on Link, I'm coming … gotta get Billy-Bob straightened out first." Link smiled.

"All right then, straighten him out…then come get me straight." He patted his crouch.

"In your dreams," she chimed sarcastically, "been there, done and not impressed."

"Oh Kirby, you cut me right to the bone. Betcha you hoping me to ask you to come back."

"Yeah, only in your dreams," she snickered.

Link answered quickly, "But we can change that, can't we?"

Suddenly the lights in the diner flickered. "Damn," the cook cursed, just as I was getting to the end." A few seconds later everything went dark. "Shit, shit, shit," he fumed.

He fumbled about in the kitchen, found a pair of battery powered lanterns and flicked them on. The lanterns gave off a pale yellow light that cast shadows throughout the diner.

Over in the booth by the front door, Billy flicked his Zippo giving off a glimmer of light around his face. "Ooooh, I'm the ghost of Sleepy Hollow," he quipped.

"Cut it out, Jimmy." Kirby pushed away from Link and turned to confront the young prankster. Holding up her coffee pot, she shielded her face from the sudden rush of wind.

With a burst of night air the door swung open and a tall dark figure stepped through the opening. He glanced around the diner then looked down at Billy. A tightlipped smile filled his face and Billy briefly smiled back.

"C'mon in stranger, I was getting ready to tell ghost stories."

Without a word, the stranger grabbed Billy by the throat pulling him out of the booth. With the strength of three men, he tossed Billy out of the way. He then approached Kirby. His thin smile turned to a big grin. Several sharp teeth protruded from the upper lip and as he got closer his massive hands reached out to grab at her arm. Screaming, she threw the coffee pot at the intruder and retreated to the back counter. Crawling up and over it, she slid behind and hid. As Link got up to confront the interloper he too was struck and tossed aside. Kirby peeked up from behind the counter's edge. 'Take the money, take it all and leave," she pleaded. But she realized that the man was not interested in money, he wanted fresh victims and as he eyed the last of the patrons she feebly blurted out, "Leave old man Loper alone. "

A late night regular of the diner, the old man sat slumped in his booth unawares of the commotion surrounding him. A pair of Wild Turkey nips sat open and drained on the table next to his coffee mug. The stranger stared at him, the smile now a gaping hole filled with sharp teeth.

Throwing his head forward, a set of stilettos sunk into the man's neck. Blood sprung like a fountain and the stranger feasted, unawares of the cook circling the counter a blade in his hand. Slinking up behind him the ex-Marine veteran used all the skills taught during his training prior to SPECIAL OPS deployment in Afghanistan.

"Ahay!" The large kitchen knife stabbed squarely into the back of the stranger. Turning to meet the challenge, he smacked the boy down with the flick of the wrist and with his free hand pulled out the blade. Smiling, he licked it clean and then threw it to the ground. The lights of the dinner flickered giving a strobe effect to the interior. In the confusion of the moment the cook struggled to his feet and retreated to the open kitchen door. As the lights recovered a young girl skipped through the diner's front door and with inhuman speed she broad-jumped nearly ten feet onto the cooks back. Her smallish set of stiletto fangs bit hard into his neck, chomping at times to get a better grip on his jugular. Feeding on the flailing body of the cook, Kirby could hear her grunting like the sound of a pig at a feeding trough. A few times, she stopped to take a long breath. As the cook fell to the floor the youngster rolled him over, putting her knee on his chest. She looked up disapprovingly. "Yuck Papa, this one's been eating lots of garlic." The blood in his artery slowed to a trickle and the young one pushed down repeatedly to increase the flow.

At the booth, the older vampire resumed feeding on the old man. Over in the corner, Billy recovered enough to get to his feet. His neck was hurting and large dark bruises appeared all along one arm. To make matters worse, a twisted ankle could barely hold his weight. Pushing through the pain, Billy resolved to fight back. He had seen the cook's stealthy attempt on the stranger and figured that another such assault was useless. Slipping awkwardly into the kitchen, he noticed a hot grease pot used for frying potatoes. Grabbing it with a pair of oven mitts he shuffled back into the service area and flung it at the stranger. The hot grease had some effect but someone grabbed him by the ankles, pulling him down. It was then that Billy new that the fight was lost as the young vampire waif retaliated.

A third assailant appeared at the door. A young man with thin build, deep gray eyes and a pale ruddy face, he looked like a monster from a 1960's Hammer film. Immediately he threw himself onto Billy. Twisting his neck until it cracked, the vampire let the carcass drop to the floor. Speaking in a gravelly voice he offered, "Here's another for you missy." The young girl looked up with blood all over her face, her tongue-lapping residue from around her mouth. She had punched through the cook's chest cavity and was hand-pumping the heart. "I've got plenty here, you take him."

Kirby stayed low behind the serving counter. She crept over to the kitchen opening and ran to the back door. It was locked and with a whimper, she dashed back behind the open serving window. Peeking above the serving station Kirby surveyed the carnage. There was only one way out of the diner. It required passing by three hungry vampires feasting on the blood of their initial victims. Kirby remembered Link. He was still out cold on the floor and she wondered if they would go for him after draining the others. They'll be coming for me too, she thought. Adrenaline pumped through her small frame. She had to save herself and try to save Link. She couldn't leave her ex-boyfriend with those monstrous fiends. She still cared for him and knew that he would have tried to protect her if he could. Kirby snuck her phone out of the purse, lying on the floor nearby. Dialing 911, she quietly gave her name and the location of the dinner. "Hello, 911?"

"Yes, what's your emergency?"

"I'm at the All-Night Diner on Gunpowder road and there are three ... a ... killers here and ... "

"You say three killers, miss? Who have they killed?"

"They're killing everyone." She snapped back. After a few questions, the dispatcher said,

"Just hang in there and we'll have the sheriff out in a jiffy."

As she flipped her phone closed, Kirby heard whispering. The vampires were talking in low voices. The young girl's high-pitched voice cracked as she spoke.

"What shall we do now?" she pleaded. The elder vampire answered thoughtfully, "There is still time before we must find shelter for the night."

He remembered passing an old abandoned train tunnel just a few hundred feet from the diner. Cold and dark, it was just the place to shelter them from the sun's deadly rays. They still had two days left before hibernation and preservation was on his mind. His eyes met the young female gathering the last drops from her prey.

"Are you still hungry my lovely? There is a fresh one hiding in the kitchen." He then turned to the other.

"Jonas, I have picked that one over there." He pointed to Link lying unconscious on the floor. The young vampire answered respectfully,
"No, you are our master; you should be the one. I am not yet ready to convey..." He stopped short and obeyed. After all they had been through, the five decade fast in an abandoned mine shaft deep in the West Virginia hills, and those last three days of feasting on human blood, they knew that they could not survive without converts. The world was changing and they needed someone of this new era to help them survive until their next awakening.

The young girl stood up from her kill and giggled as blood dripped down her tunic top. With a stern look, the elder cautioned. "Go now or I will take the woman myself."

"Oh no papa, I like feasting on girls, they're so sweet and they smell so good. That cook,...yuck, he tasted real bad. I just hate garlic."

Kirby shuddered. *Have to think fast*, she thought. Looking around she found the only item that made sense to use against vampires. A gallon of flammable degreaser sat on a shelf under the sink. Kirby slid over to the sink and pulled it out and grabbing a lighter from her purse, she poured the liquid over the floor in front of the kitchen door. She then ripped off a piece of her apron and twirled it into a tight knot around a spatula.

They had stopped talking and Kirby expected the little assailant to be coming for her any second. When the youngster bolted through the door, Kirby lit the knotted torch and quickly tossed it at her. Flames burst up around the little vampire. Screaming she cried out, "Papa, Papa, I'm on fire." As the tall vampire came to the door a second torch hit him and his grease stained clothes caught fire.

The young male vampire left Link slumped over on the floor and exclaimed, "Whoever did this ...I will tear out your heart and cut off your head." He smothered the flames on the elder who was badly burned but still alive. It was too late for the girl; she had been fried to a crisp by the intense flames.

Kirby wasn't done yet. She began tugging at the main gas line to the grill burners. Far enough away from the fire, the open line would give her time to slip out before the fumes ignited. On her third tug it broke free sending a small stream of rancid smelling natural gas into the kitchen. Figuring that she had only a minute,

Kirby jumped onto the kitchen's service counter. Quickly slipping through the pass-through Kirby darted over to the lower set the customer counter. Unaware of her presence, the male wraith continued patting down the flames on the back of his mentor. Quickly she grabbed Link and with a mighty series of tugs the waitress slid him past the kitchen opening and out the front door.

Dragging Link a safe distance, she watched as the third vampire gave up trying to douse the flames engulfing his comrade. He began searching for the unlikely heroine that had foiled their plans. Dropping to her knees, Kirby began to cry. Please don't let him look outside just yet, she prayed from within. The prayers turned to abject fear when the last vampire spotted her and Link a few yards from the front diner's open door. He made his way to the opening, his face contorted in heretical rage. Suddenly, the diner erupted in a ball of fire. Flames shot out of the windows and Kirby watched as the last monstrous adversary stood in the doorway torn literally to shreds by a thousand shards of glass. The next thing that she heard was the unearthly series of wails echoing in the cool night air as the Vampire master inside expired. All that was left was the crackle and pop from the gas generated flames licking at what was left of the building.

The Sheriff and his deputy pulled up to the burning diner. While the deputy attended to Link, sheriff Krebbs grabbed Kirby's arm. "What the hell happened in that diner missy?" Instinctively pulling away, Kirby backed up. A sudden rush of bile filled her throat. Bending over she barfed up her earlier meal and dry heaved a few times. "Give me a few moments," she demanded.

"All right young lady, but I'm guessing that those hoodlums I'm looking for had something to do with this here fire." Kirby gave the sheriff a dirty look.

"If I told you the truth, you wouldn't believe me, so let's just say that the diner was invaded by some very bad folks."

"OK then, where are they now?" he asked sternly.

The waitress bit her top lip and rolled it over her bottom one. "They got what they deserved." Kirby stood up and surveyed the damage to the diner. As the flames raged on, the town's fire trucks began to arrive. Feeling the heat on her face, Kirby let out a deep sigh of relief knowing that she did what had to be done. The others were already dead and saving Link gave her a second chance. After her brush with death she decided not to waste more time on her own petty problems. Her thoughts were interrupted briefly by the town's fire chief.

"So miss, was it a gas explosion?" Kirby's eyes met his and she nodded in the affirmative.

In his next breath he asked, "So how many victims are still in there?" She answered matter-of-factly,

"Of the living or the living dead?" Kirby Smith walked back to Link, now standing by the paramedic's truck. Stroking his long wavy brown hair she sensed something was wrong. Link was cold to the touch, his face ashen. Kirby supposed it was from the ordeal in the diner and she held his hand.

"Link you're so cold."

"Yeah, I guess I just got a chill."

"You were out for a long while," she added. Confused and disoriented, Link asked,

"Want to tell me what happened in there?"

"OK, how about this…I just saved your ass from being a vampire's late night snack. Blew up the fucking diner and killed the bastards, that's all." Link shook off his lethargy and smiled.

"Damn, girl!" He turned to look on what was left of Bailey's diner. It was then that Kirby Smith noticed the puncture wounds on his neck and the dead paramedic in the truck's cab.

"What's that on your neck?" she asked, pulling away in disgust.

"Oh, just a bite mark from one of those in the diner. Too bad I had to die but I'm glad now….feeling much better." Link turned serious. "Now I am just like them, an immortal. You can share this life." Smiling broadly, Kirby could make out a set of elongated fangs protruding from his mouth.

"Life as one of the living dead?" she asked, fearing the response.

Link's answer was short and sweet. "Yeah, if we're careful." Kirby shed a tear and as it rolled down her cheek, she felt the bite. Soon they would need to find shelter for dawn was coming… and a long sleep soon after the feeding.

THE END

O, Friend of Night

O, friend of night,

wrap your velvet fingers 'round

and whisk me to that hidden place

within the depths of this poor soul.

Press an icy tongue on willing flesh,

lick the wounds of my unworthiness

and in total darkness chill the bones

that lay beneath these covers.

Dear shadow mate,

soothe these fears by message bound

in stark relief to common sense

bearing all that can or will not be.

Befriend me in this darkest hour,

casting out those daylight demons

comforting 'til morning light returns

for you are my best and only friend.

E.W. Bonadio

A FLY IN THE SOUP

Joel Biggs was a Cajon and he loved making soup, tomato, spicy chicken noodle, French onion, and creamy potato leek soup. He especially liked making seafood gumbo, a concoction that slid down the gullet warming the innards on chilly days. On a cool breezy late-September night, Joel flopped himself onto one of the vinyl and chromed clad chairs at his fifties styled dinette table.

The apartment, a shabby two bedroom flat with small foyer and a single bath was a mere flight up from street level. It was also within a block of an accident that had been the source of Joel's present condition. His last few hours had been a nightmare and Joel sighed as he eyed the soupspoon lying on the table.

"Time for soup," he muttered. Contemplating his present state and the challenge ahead, he let out a deep guttural grunt.

"Dang, how I gonna get dat soup outta dare?" Looking over his shoulder to the pot simmering on the stove, Joel shook his head.

His right arm lay motionless, dangling by strands of tendons and chipped bone. Blood dripped freely from the open wounds and the strange odor from a serious case of road rash filled his nostrils.

"How'm I supposed to get it in da bowl? Can't lift my arm." There was not much left to his right arm and he cringed at the sight. Turning to the other one, Joel noticed his crushed left appendage.

Jokingly he observed, "Still got da tire marks on it. Musta happened after I got thrown." He sighed, remembering his exit through the open driver's side window. "Dang fool," you could' a got killed."

In the corner of the room a crusty old Hamilton mantle clock struck the hour. "One, two, three, four," he called out after each successive strike. It was four in the morning. "How long it been?" he quipped. "Nearly three hours now and still drunk as a skunk."

Joel smiled through the sudden wave of pain shooting up his crushed but serviceable arm. Breathing in the whiskey still on his breath, Joel licked at the mixture of alcohol and blood oozing from his bleeding gums. He then picked at the remains of several front teeth, the result of a violent impact with the street. Joel's nose, encrusted with small chunks of road debris, throbbed and his hand went up, gently touching it. "Oh man, dats right…now I remember…drank too dang much." He paused as if waiting for a reply from an unseen conspirator. "Geez, I should a stopped after those three shots of Jack. Momma always said three's enough son, more get you in trouble for sure." A black fly buzzed unnoticed around his right arm. After a few passes it landed on the sticky mixture of blood and tissue oozing from Joel's nearly severed right limb. Like a small vacuum it began to suck at the wet tissue and lifeblood. Then he noticed. Buggers gonna suck me dry, he thought, watching the insect hop to another wet spot on the arm. It tickled and that made Joel cringe. With a quick exhale from between puffy blood-drenched lips, Joel blasted at the pesky intruder. It flew off circling widely for a moment, and then dive-bombed its host. Joel immediately retaliated, this time more aggressively. His crushed arm swung wildly swiping at the intruder. "Ayah," he shouted in excruciating pain. As his testy nemesis flew off it circled, then perched upside down on the ceiling above the stove. Joel suddenly let out a muffled scream. Like a hot poker iron going up through his chest, the pain from the crushed arm nearly brought him to his knees. Joel grabbed onto the soupspoon, pounding it shaft first onto the table. "I'm real hurt. Gotta get to da doctor or...."

Briefly catching his breath, Biggs recovered. He pulled out a cigarette from the pack of Marlborough's on the table. Reaching for his lighter he suddenly felt bile rising up from his gut and tossed the unlit smoke. "Dat a stupid thing to do. Maybe after soup." Joel's swollen lips pursed and he spit out a few more bits of tooth shards.

Biggs paused a few moments thinking about the fly. It had temporarily given up its quest for a late night snack and that pleased him greatly. "Time for soup," he grunted. Pushing his battered body from the table, he dragged himself six difficult steps to the stove and to the soup waiting to be stirred. "That'll do," he quipped, "have some soup, then lie down and rest a bit." Something in the back of his skull told him that he must soon seek help. As he stirred the pot, Joel remembered the young girl who lived down the hall. Just three doors down, he remembered, Apartment 2-E. She'll help me pour da soup. Then reality set in as Joel questioned his current state. "Oh man, you can't go out like dis," he mumbled. "You must look a fool." Joel straightened up and shuffled over to the hallway. An old dust and grime-covered mirror framed in flaking gold leaf paint adorned the wall. The reflection startled him. "Geez-Monee, you look real bad." That was exactly what Joel's mother had said after a night out with his friends. He'd come in from a bout of drinking drenched in sweat and dirt from falling down in the grimy streets of the French Quarter. Joel remembered his mother's house, always spotless and aromatic from fresh roses and orchids.

Thinking of his boyhood home on Canal Street, he turned back to the fly. It cocked its head, seemingly staring back. Joel remembered how they used to beat back the flies invading the front porch at dusk every summer. That's where he would have his drink and desert after dinner. The thought of warm cherries nestled in a flakey piecrust and a tall iced tea made him drool. "Killed my share of em," his mama would say. "Big black buggers from the gutters down on Bourbon Street. They gotta bite like a moccasin," she'd cackle, "sent from below just to torment the Biggs family." Her next words haunted Joel for years. "Now you remember boy, them black devils, they come from Bourbon Street. It's God's way of punishing us for touching the Devil's drink."

Biggs never believed in Cajon superstitions. But deep in his young mind he always feared there might be some truth in her words. Joel did drink at home and sometimes he'd sit out on the porch with a butterfly net catching those big horseflies. He'd douse some in bourbon or pull their wings off and stick them into a shoe polish lid he used as an ashtray. Then he'd poke their torn bodies with lit cigarettes until they stopped squirming. Thinking back on it now, Biggs longed for to those lazy days of summer. Joel smiled at the mental picture of dead flies in his makeshift ashtray. He longed for a sip of bourbon and a smoke - but first comes the soup.

"Oh mama, if you could see me now," he opined, his head throbbing from the spirits she had railed against. Joel Biggs rebelled at nineteen and his troubles came from more than catching and torturing flies. Soon after entering college, Joel took up with Jerry Stubbs, a high school friend and a part time dogcatcher. The animal shelter truck was free transportation for a poor college kid and together they began drinking in it as they drove the city streets looking for a good time. They quickly turned to snaring stray cats and dogs and drowning them in a nearby lake just for fun.

Eventually, his lust for torture got Joel seven days in lockup for killing a neighbor's pet, a nasty miniature poodle with an attitude. Joel would have gotten away with it except that its owner noticed him snagging the dog. When they came to question him Joel broke down, admitting his involvement. But Joel quickly found an ally in his mother. "It was a mercy killing," she had said. "The dog was a pest, tearing up flower beds all along our street." She was there at the arraignment, still defending her son.

"He's a good boy your honor, he just needs to stay off the spirits."

When he turned twenty-six Joel made what he thought was

a life changing decision. He moved up to Memphis, taking a job as a cook. Biggs soon learned the art of making mouth-watering soups from a bayou bred brown-skinned beauty he met at the diner. Corrine was a waitress but her home-schooled recipes for soup were outstanding. Joel used her soup recipes to make his mark and in gratitude he asked her and her sister to move in with him in the second floor apartment.

Old habits die-hard and Joel soon became bored with his new career and chatty girlfriend. He wanted more than what Corrine could give and fell back on old habits, shots of Jack Daniels with beer chasers. With each new day the alcohol's hold on him became stronger. It ended with Corrine when she caught him drunk in the apartment, fondling her twelve-year-old sister. Her revenge was swift. Corrine's written recipes that had made Joel successful. Without them he was lost.

That night Corrine snuck into the diner's kitchen, grabbed the recipes and tossed a handful of dead flies into Joel's soup stock. By that next afternoon, Joel was fired. Without a reference and her recipes to fall back on Joel became just another unemployed drunk. Biggs apologized to Corrine. "I'm gonna change back, honest, just don't leave me." His words fell on deaf ears and as she packed up to leave Corrine cautioned, "Joel, It'll get you to real trouble someday…might just get you killed."

With the tip end of an umbrella retrieved from the hallway stand, Biggs poked at gooey strands of matted hair. He flicked the loose bangs back over his bloody brow and starred back into his two swollen eye sockets. "Dang sight," he remarked squinting hard to better focus below on his nose and mouth. There was large gash running down his left cheek. "No matter," he noted matter-of-factly. Biggs heaved a half-hearted sigh. "Dang hungry....need soup...that'll make me feel better." Pensively he nodded, "Once I've et, I'll go down to 2-E and ask the lady... take me to hospital. But Biggs didn't know her name. He had seen her a few times, exchanging smiles and waves, but never got up the nerve to invite her over. An updated the list of tenants with their phone numbers had recently been delivered. "Where's dat list?" he quipped. "Ah there it is." Reaching the table near the front door Joel thumbed down the page. "Suzie Kurtz, that's her." Nodding, he made a mental note to call her after his meal.

Joel didn't notice the pesky black fly as it flew down from the ceiling. He also didn't notice the others congregating along the half-open window of his second story flat. Soon dozens more made their way into the apartment, their sensory orbs attracted to the open wounds of the unsuspecting host. Feeling better, he dragged himself over to the stove leaving a trail of blood and a basket weave pattern behind. As Biggs looked back at the mosaic of blood he commented, "Cool. I gotta show dis to someone."

Joel stepped away from the unintended floor art. "Soup time," he blurted out, announcing his intentions to the bevy of unseen guests. Biggs slowly made his way over to the stove. Still very drunk and nearly cathartic from his serious injuries, he used every ounce of strength to accomplish the task. Lifting the top of the pot he breathed in the sweet smell of tomato, herbs and spices.

The pain from deep cuts, crushed bones and internal

trauma had temporarily subsided. But as he bent over the pot Joel lost vision as his right eye slipped from its swollen socket. Swearing he muttered, "Damnation!"

He thought back to earlier that night, why he was in such a poor condition. Biggs recalled drinking at the bar. He remembered staggering over to the truck and turning over the ignition, then nothing until the crash. The truck had hit a high curb at forty-five miles an hour. Too late to adjust the wheel, it had flipped over. Unbelted, Biggs exited the driver's side window, rolling into the path of an oncoming car.

Joel remembered the headlights coming at him and the thump, cracking of bone and pain as it rolled over his arm. Bastard didn't even stop, he thought, his mind now focused on the crushed arm. Oh well, safe for the moment, Biggs thought as he turned the burner knob to the off position. "OK, soup's ready," he purred.

An impressive new army of invaders had successfully made it through the open window; big black flies, hungry and unafraid, some with breeding intentions. They sensed the feast to come, not only from Joel's soup, but also his flesh, organs, and blood. The smell of the tomato soup lingered heavily in the air and thousands of tiny eyes focused on the pot while a horde of others kept watch on the host, a broken drunk happily stirring the liquid below. A few interlopers now took to settling on the stove, a well-worn four burner electric range. The more aggressive ones set down on the pot cover in plain view. They hip-hoped around the rim dancing like tiny Indians preparing for war. Some took to licking at the cooling residue slurped onto its edge.

As Joel churned the pot, he spotted them. "Get you gone," he bellowed. A hard stream of spittle and blood spewed out from his mouth spraying over the range, some into the cooling soup. Most of Joel's adversaries fled, quickly settling nearby to reform for a second advance. With his one useable eye, Biggs jerked around preparing a counter to the next assault. Using his more serviceable left arm, Joel reluctantly grabbed a ladle and began pouring the soup into a bowl nestled on the counter. Only half of each scoop made it into the bowl. Joel didn't care; he would have his bowl of soup, and then deal with the flies. Biggs needed soup and after the night he'd experienced, a few flies were not going to stop him. It was not a quest but a challenge of sorts and his adversaries, the flies, would be denied the spoils of war.

There were now several hundred of the winged terrors scrumming for a meal. They swarmed around Joel's head, taunting him, buzzing fiercely as he ladled the soup. Biggs continued, stopping from time to time to swat at the aggressors. "Ayah," he cried out as the last ladle caught a fly swimming leisurely in the creamy brick-red mixture.

"Dat's it," he snarled, "no more nice guy!" Joel put the ladle down and hunched over. Opening up the base cabinet next to the stove, he found a sixteen-ounce can of super strong bug killer. "Take dat," he snarled as the little black spray cap opened up a swath of pesticide into the room. Flies darted back and forth, some spinning out of control like gunned down aircraft on their way to oblivion. Thirty flies died in the first counter attack. Twenty-five more hit the floor, legs twitching briefly until dead. "Got you on the run now," he snarled.

Joel sprayed the entire room until the can ran out but still the army of flies could not be deterred. He choked, coughing up gobs of blood, which spread over his tan shirt like paintball splatter. The deadly fumes had taken their toll both on the flies and Biggs. He began to feel dizzy and swayed, glassy-eyed for a few moments. Falling to the floor in a heap, he passed out. Hours later Biggs regained consciousness. His one good eye opened and as he scanned the room he could feel them, thousands of little critters crawling, jumping and buzzing around his head. The clock began to strike the hour and through the pain, Joel counted the hours- six, seven, eight, nine o'clock. The soup, he remembered, and in a fit of rage Biggs pulled his battered body off the floor. Now on his knees, Joel noticed only one arm hanging from his torso. The other lay in a heap, an inanimate piece of humanity now on the floor covered with flies. They danced about in a victory celebration. But their victory was not complete. Biggs still had life and as long as he did, he'd fight.

"Stubborn flies, I killed a bunch of you dead, now I'm gonna get the rest of ya." Joel slid one knee after the other until he came back to the open base cabinet that housed cleaning products and paint cans. From within, a large can of brush cleaner caught his one good eye. "That'll do," he chirped. Pulling out the can, he held the cap between his broken teeth and gradually twisted his jaw until the top flopped onto the floor. The sound sent his adversaries into frenzy. They swarmed over to the cabinet, setting down in mass. Thousands of fly eyes now watched his every move. "You gonna get it now," he swore. Knocking the can over, Joel let the liquid flow out onto the tile. It covered the area around him and he screamed out as the petroleum based cleaner soaked into his open wounds. "Oh crap!" he exclaimed. Sliding away from the mixture, Biggs regained composure just as a new swarm of avengers came down from above, their suckers picking at the exposed eyeball, and Joel's open mouth. Gagging from the mass of attackers piling down his throat Jason stuck his hand inside, pulling out many of the squiggly pests. The rest he reluctantly gulped down. Biggs reached into his shirt pocket and retrieving his cigarette lighter, he flicked it with no result. Biggs began to panic. Flick, flick, flick – there was still no spark. The flies began to close in again, mercilessly picking at his open wounds. Joel could see some of them laying eggs and he shuddered at the thought. Three times more the lighter flicked. On the last strike a spark flickered. With a sudden flash the chemical exploded setting the room ablaze, flame and smoke quickly rising to the ceiling. "Yeah!" Biggs howled as the army of flies retreated. His clothes had briefly caught fire but flamed out during the melee. Pain from burns eased as the accelerant burned out and again Biggs passed out. As time passed a new hoard of pests arrived.

Led by a freakishly large creature with satin black body and translucent wings decorated in swirls of red and green they poured through the open window. It was the demon fly of Joel's nightmare, huge crimson red eyes swiveling about surveying the apartment landscape. The monster's wings spread out in defiance, its prickly barbed legs pulsing up and down, signaling commands to the horde at its disposal. This was the cursed demon spirit Joel's mother spoke of in evening chats about the perils of alcohol.

The next thing that Joel Biggs remembered was the knock at his apartment door. Somewhere from below a siren sounded. It quickly went silent. As he awoke from his stupor, Joel realized he was still alive. The apartment fire had long since burned out. His last ditch effort was a stroke of genius and he had survived the last stand against the horde of flies. There was no major damage to the room except for a badly singed cabinet and several blistered floor tiles. Joel had won his battle for superiority. It was man over nature.

"Oh Geez, the soup," he groused. From outside the apartment someone called out.

"Hey in there, you OK?"

"Yeah, yeah," Biggs responded, "wait a minute?" Slowly rising up off the floor, Joel pulled his body to the open base cabinet. The bowl of tomato soup was right there where he had left it to do battle with the flies.

Again someone shouted, "Hey, if you don't open up, we'll have to knock the door down?" Joel smirked thinking what else could possibly go wrong. He had gotten drunk, hit a curb, gotten thrown out of his truck, run over by a car, lost an arm, and was attacked by thousands of flies. Biggs had burned himself nearly to a crisp, and now someone was going to break down his apartment door. "Then what," he asked himself, "will they cart me away in a straightjacket?"

"I'm all right...just another minute." Joel did not notice the black cloud of flies covering the ceiling, waiting patiently for their leader's signal.

Joel stood up as straight as he could manage, grabbed the soup, and shuffled over to the table. Gingerly, Biggs set the bowl down and flopped into the chair. He felt no pain now; didn't even think beyond the first spoon of elixir. Biggs would have his soup and nothing would stop him, not even the men outside threatening to break down the door. Someone called out, this time a young woman's voice from beyond the door.

"Mr. Biggs, its Suzie, Suzie Kurtz. Please open the door." Startled, Joel turned to the melodic tone.

"Thanks but I'm trying to eat my soup." Joel thought of Corrine and how good she was to him before he let her down. He wondered if Suzie could take her place and vowed to change if she'd have him. But the woman would first have to prove herself. "You can take me to hospital after I've had soup." As Joel began to eat, they attacked."

The banging returned, this time more forceful and a voice from beyond the locked door said, "I think the guy in there is crazy. Let's break the sucker down."

Joel continued to eat his soup with an occasional stir to blend the slimy mixture of blood, soot, flecks of ceiling paint, and spittle.

"Looks good," he crowed. "Bona Petite!" Each time Joel tried to slurp his soup he dribbled a mixture blood, dead flies, and mucus. Taking each mouthful, he gulped hard and gasped. Moments later the door to apartment 2-A burst open.

Two burly firemen entered, searching for evidence of a fire. Puzzled by the foul smell, scores of dead flies, and bloodstains, they searched through the debris. Joel's detached arm lay in a heap and the first fireman poked at it. From within the mess of tissue and remnant of Joel's s shirtsleeve, a mass of flies erupted. They scattered, quickly finding the open window. The curious neighbor from 2-E followed behind the second firemen, holding tightly onto his coat sleeve. She looked over his shoulder at the disgusting carnage and the figure sitting at the table.

"I think that's Mr. Biggs over there," she said, pointing in his direction. Biggs turned from the table offering a grotesque toothless smile.

"Come on in, I'd offer you some, but there's still flies in my soup." The young woman screamed as hundreds of maggots wiggled out from inside of the dying man's half-open shirt. Joel could barely hold up his soupspoon. On it the devil horsefly perched, its head a mass of multifaceted sensory cells. The elongated snout quivered as it sucked down the last of the soup on the spoon. Then it dashed away leading thousands of its cohorts through the apartment window. Their work finished, the curse had run its course.

As the last of the winged intruders exited Biggs began to vomit, convulsing, his regurgitated soup a feast for the larva deposited hours before. The first fireman called down for the paramedics waiting below. "You boys need to come up her now...looks like you got a mess to clean up." During his last moments of life, Biggs could hear the EMT's talking.

"It's a shame, and just a few blocks away from the hospital," one said.

"Yeah, a shame." the other replied shaking his head, "Guess he's just crazy drunk. I can't figure how he ever made it up to the apartment, what with his arms crushed and head beat up and all."

Looking down at Biggs, the first man considered, "A strong bugger though, don't you think. Drunks just don't know any better."

"I vote for crazy," the other countered. "Crazies can get pretty strong too...must've been really hungry for soup."

"What about all the flies those firemen said was feeding on him? Where'd they go?"

"Beats me," the other said shrugging his shoulders, "except for the dead ones and these here maggots." Still in his latex gloves, he picked at the larva in Joel's open wounds.

"Yeah," the other winced, "Just looking for a free meal I guess."

Turning away he added, "What a way to go, eh?"

As the ambulance began to drive away, Suzie Kurtz stood in the apartment building doorway. Still in shock from the traumatic scene in apartment 2-A, she pulled out a pack of cigarettes. Lighting up Suzie watched the huge winged creature at the head of a swarm of flies following close behind. At the light the ambulance turned followed only by the winged leader. The mass of insects left behind scattered, drifting up and away over the buildings.

THE END

Shot Through the Heart

She sat on the edge of the bed, tears in her eyes, and a spattering of blood on her hands. The cell phone on the nightstand rang out the Stevie Wonder song - You are the sunshine of my life. It was Valentines Day and her husband had come for a brief conjugal visit.

"Hello, mother, yes, I'm OK." A long pause followed. "Yeah I did it, killed him dead just like you said I should. Shot him right through the heart...just like you said."

The caller squawked back and she cringed. Alice Crowley stood up and walked over to the window. "Yes mother, the police are outside, called them right after. I know what to say. He beat me and I shot him in self defense." They were coming now, at the front door. The chime from the doorbell rang out and Alice slipped on her robe and slippers. As she made her way down the stair, Alice thought of the last few days with Josh Crowley. There was no life with a man like Josh, a thief, murderer, and womanizer who disappeared for weeks, returning only when he needed a place to hide from the law. Alice would remember to tell that to the police. They'd see that it had to be done.

As the front door opened a pair of serious looking patrolmen appeared. "You OK miss?" one of them asked. "Oh yes, I think...think so." She stuttered.

The other chimed in, "you called about a shooting incident?"

"Yes, it's my husband, I shot my husband in the bedroom."

"Where's the weapon?"

"Oh, I don't...I think it's upstairs on the bed."

Pushing their way through the door they looked around for evidence of others in the home.

"Anyone else here lady?"

"Oh no, we live here alone," she replied.

From upstairs a voice called out, "Who is it dear?"

Alice turned to the sound and nearly fainted.

"Is that your husband, maam?"

"Ugh, Oh, yes but...." She couldn't believe her ears. He was dead when she left him in the blood-soaked bed, eyes rolled back in his head. It can't be, she thought.

Together, they started up the stairs, the two policemen first with Alice following behind, scared and confused by the sound of her husband's voice. As they reached the top, Josh Crowley stormed out of the bedroom, a gun in his hand. Immediately, he pointed it at the men. Before the officers could react shots rang out and both fell back, crashing down the narrow open staircase. Alice held onto the banister avoiding them as they fell. As she recovered on the staircase, Josh pointed the gun at her.

"So, you called the cops so soon after I came back for some lovin and a few beers? Hey, it's Valentines Day sweetie." His face contorted. "I had a surprise for you too, but I don't know if you deserve it now."

She didn't know what to say; she didn't want to die. "Oh, Josh, I didn't mean to shoot you. Mother made me do it."

Josh laughed. "Oh, don't worry about this little thing." He stuck his index finger into the hole in his chest. Pulling it out, he showed her a crimson red-coated digit. "It'll heal, just need to plug it up 'till my body heals."

Alice's eyes widened and she gasped. "Your not gonna kill me are you?"

"Why do you think that," he laughed, "Its Valentines Day and I had a surprise for you." His eyes widened and a big smirk appeared. "Now where's that mother of yours? She's been a bad girl and I'm gonna punish her for trying to get me killed."

"Oh, I don't know Josh, probably at home watching the Late Show," she mused still scared to death at the sight of her husband, a bullet hole in his chest and a big smile on his face.

"Why do you want to know?"

"Call her and ask her to come over. I think we should have a little talk." He looked over at the two dead policemen. We need to get these boys up and seated for the show. No need to have them bleeding all over the floor."

Alice could not fathom what he might be up to but nodded, "OK, I'll call mother now. She pulled out the cell phone from the pocket of her robe while Josh retrieved the dead patrolmen. Pulling them over to the dinning room off the foyer, Josh propped them up as best he could. "There you go boys, right smart looking." He arranged their caps just right and wiped the blood off their foreheads. "Now you look like real smart cops."

Alice dialed the number. Three rings later her mother answered. "Yes Alice, how's it going?" She waited for a reply but none came. "Have they called the coroner yet?"

"No mother, there's been a development." Alice didn't want Josh to hear the fear in her voice. "Josh killed them and he's waiting for you to come over."
"What? I thought......"

"Look mother, you had better get over here. I need you to..."

"OK, just sit tight. I'll finish off the SOB. You just keep him occupied until I get there."

"I will mother, please hurry, I'm real scared," she whispered.

After Josh finished arranging the table he drifted into the kitchen. As she hung up the phone he called back to her, "Want a beer Alice?"

"No, no thanks." She was shaking uncontrollably. How did he survive the gunshot, she thought. I must find out how he's alive with a hole in his chest. What was he up to? Her questions were soon answered.

Josh came out, a beer in his hand and a dish cloth sticking out of his chest. "Had to plug this up. No sense letting my blood drip all over the place." He smiled again. "Oh don't worry Alice, It's healing up real good." He pulled the cloth out and spread his shirt apart revealing the hole in his chest closing up and hair growing over the spot. Pulling off his shirt, Josh turned his back to her. "How's the exit hole healing up?"

Alice stood dumbfounded as she watched skin grafting over the wound. "How is this happening?"

"Oh, I never told you that I've been given the power to heal myself."

"What? How can that be?" He sat her down at the table across from the dead policemen.

"It happened last year when I helped an old Gypsy woman. She was being mugged and I caught the little punks in the act. Gutted one and broke the other's arm. They didn't put up much of a fight but I did get slashed up a bit."

"So she gave you a special healing poultice or something like that?"

"No, even better, she prayed a few strange prayers over my wounds and cast a spell. Since that time I can now heal myself of any wound."

"So you can't be killed?"

Oh, I can be killed, but only by my own hand. That's what she said. I can kill myself when I choose and I'll always have an out, like if they put me in prison or I get too old and can't do for myself anymore." He looked at her with big grin on his face.

"So tell me, why did you shoot me in my sleep?" He knew the answer but wanted her to come clean with him.

"Mother said that our marriage was a sham and that I needed to do you in before they arrest me for accessory to your terrible crimes."

"Oh, so your mother wants me out of the picture, does she?

Well we'll just have a little talk with mommy when she get's here."

Alice had seen that look in Josh's face before. He meant to kill her mother, possibly her as well. "Now Josh, it is Valentines Day and you didn't even get me a present did you?"

He laughed, "Well, I'm not gonna forgive you for trying to kill me, how's that for starters. I did get you something." He got up and strode over to the hall table. Pulling out the small center drawer, Josh pulled out a box and threw it over to her. "Here, sweetie, don't ever say I never cared."

Alice opened the box. Inside she found a gold broach covered with diamonds and rubies. "Oh Josh it's beautiful." Alice decided that her only chance was to give herself to him, if only for one more night.

"Yeah, I did all right didn't I?"

Alice put it on and walked over to him. "I love it Josh." She pulled him to her and kissed him hard. "Sorry that I tried to kill you but mother..."

"That's Ok Alice." Suddenly he pushed her away. "Happy Valentines Day!" He pulled out the gun that she had used on him. "Sorry sweetie but you gotta go now. I'll make it fast though." As he aimed at her ashen face, Alice's mother burst through the door. Immediately, she grabbed at his gun. As Josh tried to twist it away, his finger slipped and a shot rang out striking him in the head.

He fell to the floor, the gun still in his hand and Alice screamed, "No mother, he's just gonna keep coming back." As they watched him bleeding from the gunshot Alice told her mother of Josh's story of the Gypsy woman.

"Only by his hand," she had said.

Ten minutes went by and still Josh did not move. Alice called 911 and asked for assistance. "Please hurry," she said, "There are two dead policemen and I'm afraid that my husband will come back from the dead to kill me."

"OK lady, just what have you been drinking tonight?"

When the second police unit arrived they took Alice and her mother in for questioning. Hours later they were booked for homicide. She had no answer for who had killed the two policemen answering her call earlier that night. Her mother, booked for murder, could not answer why her fingerprints were on the weapon that killed Josh Crowley.

THE END

THE ODD JOB

Gordon Pike needed a job. It had been six months since being laid off from his mid-five figure sales gig. But Gordon understood that keeping busy was the ticket to success, that and getting out of the house before his money crazy wife nagged him to death. Pouring through the want ads at a local bar, the thirty-six year old college graduate found several jobs, automotive associate, copy machine sales, water filtration systems rep, and other less than exciting ways of making a living. Depressed and in need of a new beginning, Gordon began scouring the section marked, 'Personal Help'.

"Ah, this looks interesting," he cooed folding down the newspaper to read the single-spaced offering: Stimulating job experience for a person with exceptional patience and a willing attitude.

Sitting in a booth behind Gordon, a pair of young girls giggled. Turning around with a scowl he quipped, "What's so funny?"

"Oh, nothing, we were just wondering if you were rich or married. You look so distinguished."

Sticking up his left hand, Gordon flashed his wedding ring. "Yeah, I'm married, but don't let that stop you from wondering if I'd cheat. I won't, not yet ...can't afford it 'till I get a job."

They smirked and the younger one, a pretty blonde answered, "Well, when you do get some money please give me a call. I'm sure we could work something out." She slipped a piece of paper over the top of the booth. Tossing her hair back, she winked.

"My fee is quite reasonable." They stood up and from the look of them Gordon could tell that they were working girls. Oh great, he thought, propositioned by a prostitute who wants money that I don't have. Laughing, he went back to reading the help wanted ad.

Man Wanted

Bright and energetic young man

Must be physically fit and possess strong spirit

Personal attendant to a retired industrialist

Long term position with excellent pay

Call for in-person interview

Immediate start.

Gordon had only one concern, how much money would the old geezer pay and for what services? After the episode the prostitutes he wondered if the old guy was a rich pervert looking for a young stud.

"Yuck, he cringed, "I could never do that, even for an hour, not with a man." Calling home, he offered an excuse.

"Hey Doris, I got this interview in a bit. It could be a good gig and I could start right away so don't make dinner." The voice on the other end of the line squawked, "Well don't expect much when you get home. I can't work, take care of the house and cook for you. Maybe you should eat out tonight. Besides, I'm going out with the girls...should be home by ten."

Gordon slammed the cell phone shut. He scowled briefly, and then stuck up his middle finger shoving it defiantly toward the inanimate object.

"I'll show you...get that job, get a bunch of money and then I'll call that prostitute...do the nasty all night long. Yeah, that's what I'll do." He studied the number written on the scrap of paper salivating at the thought. Slipping back into reality, Pike opened up his cell phone and dialed the number listed on the help wanted ad. Three rings into the call a woman answered,

"Hell...hello, can I help you," she stuttered.

"Yes, I'm calling about the job listed in the paper."

"Oh my, I believe that position has been filled."

Gordon swore under his breath but recovered quickly,

"Are you sure?" The voice in the phone stuttered again,

"Well...well, I...I think ssss.so, but give me a minute." She left the phone and Gordon could hear a voice in the background.

"Tell him to come anyway dear."

Pike smiled to himself. Gotta make this work for me, he thought. He wanted this job even though there was yet no talk of money. When she returned, the lady offered him the address and said, "Please come as soon as possible mister...."

"Pike misses, Gordon Pike. I'll be there within an hour."

Forty-five minutes later Gordon Pike was at the front of an old mansion in the most prestigious section of town. The massive front gates of the compound were closed but an intercom protruded from a post at the curb. Pushing on the call button, Gordon announced, "Hello, this is Gordon Pike. I'm out at the front gates."

He waited but no answer came back. Suddenly the gates parted. The initials above the separated gate arms – LM caught his attention and he wondered aloud, "Lawrence Mellon?" The road inside snaked around and to the right past a small carriage house and several hedgerows. He began walking up the drive and was met by an old man in a fully decked out golf cart. "Get in...Mister Pike isn't it?"

"Yes sir," was all Gordon could say.

"Pleased to meet you...I'm Lawrence Mellon and this is my home."

"Yes sir, I figured that out." Gordon looked around as he sifted the name around in his brain. "You are the man who made all that money during the alternative energy boom, right?"

"Among other investments," he replied. I'm impressed with you already." Gordon perked up.

"Well, everyone around here has heard of your renewable auto battery system. It has been a real boon to solving gas shortages worldwide."

"Yes, I've been working on such things recently....knew that it would pay off someday, but I'm too old to enjoy the fruits of my labor. Not into travel so I stay at home preoccupied with my hobbies."

"I'm pleased to make your acquaintance, sir. It's an honor." Gordon tried to be words genuine. He wanted to get the lay of the land, to find out how much the job paid before committing.

Inside the mansion, Mellon shuffled Pike into a massive library filled with hundreds of books. They shelves covered the well lit room nearly sixteen feet high. A tall ladder system had been installed to reach the top tier of shelves and Pike stood silently gazing at it. Mellon watched as the young man stood amazed at the myriad of books. "Yes son, these are all my books, meticulously collected over fifty years."

"Wow sir, I've never seen so many books, even in my hometown library."

"Don't worry Mr. Pike; the job does not include handling these books. This is only where I interview prospects."

"OK sir, I'm ready, here is my resume and...."

"No need Gordon; I have a good feeling about you. You seem straight as an arrow to me. That's all I need for now." He looked over to the doorway leading into the hall and smiled as a lady dressed in flowing white gown glided into the room. She was quite old, at least seventy. The skin on her face had been stretched by several facelifts. Gordon could tell that she was once beautiful, but the years had taken their toll.

"Gordon, meet my wife, Emily." Mellon took his wife's wrinkled hand and placed it in Gordon's.

"Pleased," he said, quickly removing his hand. She smiled thinly and Pike could see that she was disappointed. Oh no, he thought, now I've done it, dissed the old gal and probably lost any chance of getting the job.

Mellon asked him to sit and Gordon picked a large wing chair nearby. "Want a drink, Gordon? We have anything you might desire, Gin, Vodka, Bourbon..." The old man's voice trailed off.

"A...no thanks, sir."

Mellon looked pleased. "Good, good, I like a man who has the power to say no to alcohol; dulls one's manhood if you know what I mean. Now let's get down to business. I want to make a proposition. You see we did just hire someone for the job offered in the paper. However, there is another service that you may be capable of providing. It pays more but is only a temporary position."

Gordon became excited. "How much more?"

"I like a man who get's right to the point. How about one thousand dollars per hour? There would be a minimum of six hours per week, or more if requested. Of course this is a cash only transaction and it requires that you are available on notice twenty-four hours every day rain or shine, holiday or not."

Gordon Pike nearly jumped out of his seat. "Yes sir, I'll take it."

"Wait a minute son, I hadn't told you yet what the job entails."

"Don't care sir, I'll do anything."

"Anything?"

"Yep, for that kind of money, I'd shovel crap from every crapper in this mansion."

"Not necessary Gordon, all you have to do is be available when my wife needs your services. You see, I'm too old and too weak to keep up with her. She's a veritable dynamo and her appetite is far too aggressive for this feeble soul." He smiled broadly. "We've had a good life together, but what you see around you is my world. Lady Mellon is part of a different world. If you take the job you will see."

Gordon felt ill. He wondered, What have I gotten myself into? But he needed the money. If he could make it through the next few weeks, he'd be on easy street. With all the down time he'd still have time to look for a proper job. Looking over at Mellon's smiling wife, Gordon got a chill up his back. She gave him a wink just like the cute young prostitute he had encountered. Then he thought of the original job. "What about the other guy? Maybe he would switch with me?"

"Oh, I never thought of that Gordon. You know, I might just be wiling to make the switch. His job only pays one hundred an hour but it is a full time position. Are you certain that you want to switch?"

"Ah… yeah, I have no stomach for sex. My wife even says I'm no good at it so I don't think I would be a good partner for your lovely wife." He looked over to the woman with pleading eyes. "Maam, you understand don't you?"

She stammered, "Lawrence, I hope you...you can talk...talk him into this. I...I want him even for just one d.d.dday."

Mellon groused, "All right dear, I'm sure that Mr. Pike will be willing to spend an hour with you for a few thousand dollars." He turned to Gordon. "Right mister Pike?"

Gordon began to sweat profusely. A few thousand for an hour or so, he thought? Why not? "Ok, you win Mellon; I'll do it for three thousand right now in my hand."

Mellon called for his manservant and asked for the money from his personal safe. When he returned with the cash, Gordon took the money. "Now what?" Shifting his feet like he had been stepping on hot coals, Gordon Pike waited for the inevitable instructions.

Mellon directed his manservant, "Take Mister Gordon to Emily's special place." As he walked behind the man, Gordon struck up a conversation. "So what's it like, being the love slave of a rich woman?" The prim and proper manservant shot him a look of disdain.

"How would I know sir, that is not my job here at the mansion." He led Pike up to a second floor wing of the mansion. It was decidedly decadent, deep red covered walls and low lighting. Pictures of men and women in various states of sexual intercourse lined the walls. At the end of the hallway, there were two ornate doors decorated with gold leaf embossments depicting grotesque forms of both men and women. Opening it, the manservant ushered Pike into the room.

"Oh my God!" he exclaimed. Inside, a large round bed sat centered in the room. Various contraptions lay around, some looking more like dark-age implements of torture. A cage with a strategically placed hole used for inserting one's manhood got his immediate attention. Over in a corner, a whipping post with chains and a cat-o-nine tails gave him the shivers. And in an opposite corner Gordon spied a glass tank filled with a jelly-like substance. There were all manner of hoods, masks and devilish sex toys strewn about the room and Pike felt the sudden urge to flee.

"You are free to examine anything in the room sir but please don't leave. Mrs. Mellon will be up directly." With a nod, the manservant closed the doors behind Pike. He was now alone but deep within, a strange excitement took hold. He thought what if she just wants to play? I can do that, but no rough stuff. Wandering around the room Pike began to let his mind drift. He thought of the two young prostitutes and wished that it were they that he was to service. The money still burned into his mind and Gordon vowed to make the most of the time.

As he fingered the holes in the leather head gear draped over the whipping post, Mrs. Mellon appeared. Dressed in an elegant nightgown that must have cost them thousands, she smiled. "Like my little toys Gordon?"

"Ah, yes, very interesting," he countered, putting down the headgear.

"So, what shall we do first?" she asked. Moving over to the bed, Emily Mellon began to undress. First the sheer covering, then a series of undergarments, She pulled off her diamond earrings, let down her thin gray locks and bid him to come to her. Gordon sheepishly moved closer.

"Take off your clothes Gordon," she demanded. He obliged. Standing stark naked, Gordon Pike felt more vulnerable than at any time in his life. Impressed by the sight of him, Emily turned to a small writing desk and retrieved a document. Turning back to him Emily presented the paper and a pen. "Please sign this." It was a contract with payment terms and a non disclosure agreement.

"What's this?" he pressed.

"Never you mind Gordon, just sign the paper."

"I'll need to read it over first," he answered.

"No, sign this now or forfeit the money," she responded. The piercing stare told him that she was serious. Gordon needed the money and after a few tense moments, he took the papers and signed.

"Now we will have some fun," she quipped. Gordon closed his eyes and she led him to the bed. Nearly two hours later, sickened and ashamed, Gordon Pike left the mansion. After the unpleasant experience, Pike had only one out, to change places with the other man hired before he was exposed to Emily Mellon. Gordon decided that he'd return and plead for the switch.

It was a fretful night. Although flush with money, Gordon could not repeat his escapade with Lady Mellon. Returning home to a suspicious wife, Gordon Pike revealed the pile of cash. She hugged him hard and squealed. "Let's go out and celebrate." Exhausted and in no mood for partying, he flopped in a chair.

"No thanks, I'm real tired; maybe tomorrow night. I'll be more inclined to party then." He got up and trudged to the bathroom. After a long hot shower he was in bed, but the vile and disgusting manner in which he allowed himself to be used stayed with him. When she came to bed, Gordon's wife flopped playfully and cuddled. Purring sweetly in his ear she said, "C'mon, let's play."

"No, please, I can't tonight," he begged; gotta get some rest."

"Ok, but I want a few hundred for shopping?" Pike nodded, "OK, now please let me sleep." He tried but could not immediately get comfortable. Several hours passed before he finally dozed off.

The next morning Pike's cell phone rang. Opening it, Gordon realized that it was Mellon. "Oh Geez," he said, "Here we go again." Pulling on his pants, Gordon retrieved a fresh shirt, pulled on a pair of socks and donned his black oxfords.

"Gotta go," he shouted as he rushed out the door. On the way to the mansion, Gordon decided to just go for it and demand the switch of jobs. Once at the mansion's gate he settled down, calling into the intercom. "Hello, this is Gordon Pike out here at the gate." Moments later, Mellon's manservant arrived in the golf cart. The gates opened.

"Nice to have you back Mr. Pike."   "Yeah, well I did sign those papers.

"Papers?" the man answered quizzically.

"Yes, the one that Emily Mellon had me sign."

"Oh sir, I'm shocked that you would sign such an agreement. Didn't you read the terms?"

"Ah, sure, it was just basic stuff like how much money and that I'd be on call and...." His voice suddenly trailed off. "Oh God, what else was in there?"

"Well sir, you singed on to five years with forfeiture of all monies if you break the contract."

Gordon's eyes widened. "Now wait a minute, I was told that I might have a chance to switch with the other guy who got the first offer."

"Yes, well I suppose you can switch, but unlike you, Mr. Jenkins did not sign a long term contract. He agreed to stay on for three days and will be discharged from his duties with no penalty after completing the term. If you persist in making the switch, you will have to honor the agreement for the entire time of employment."

"Sure, but I still want to make the switch. Jenkins will only have to service the old lady for two more days. That should be a cakewalk for him."

When they arrived at the mansion Gordon perked up and strolled confidently into the library. Old man Mellon was waiting for him, a curious look on his face.

"Sit down mister Pike," he asked. In his hand was the contract that Gordon had signed. "I believe you signed this document?" Gordon answered smugly, "Yep, signed it yesterday."

"So you know that you are committed to be in our employ for five years, correct?"

"Guess so, at the rate that you stated."

"All right then, but what's this I hear that you want to switch duties with Jenkins?"

"Yes, no hard feelings but I can't commit to the job I did yesterday, especially for five years. No offense, but Mrs.

Mellon may not last that long. Still, I can't take the chance." Mellon put his fingers up to his chin, drumming in meditation.

"All right, I'll honor your request and make the switch, but I can tell you, Mrs. Mellon will be quite displeased. I wish that you would reconsider."

"No chance, my mind is made up." Gordon suddenly got a strange sinking feeling in his gut as Mellon brought over a contract addendum.

"Now by signing this, you agree to a switch of duties but there is one catch." Pike shook his head, "And that is?"

"You cannot break the covenant. You must also forgo all ties to the outside world. As of this moment you will live full time at the mansion, not to leave the grounds for any reason. The penalty for attempting to leave is the forfeiture of all money. There are also other more severe penalties for disobeying your duties."

"OK, so let me get this straight, I must leave my wife?"

"Yes, once you sign on, you must stay on the grounds for five years, never to leave, even for conjugal visits." He turned to the window. "Just as John has served me in his own way, you will attend to my every whim." Turning back to Gordon, Mellon waited for a reply."

"And once signed, I will receive the money as promised?"

"Yes, it will go directly into a personal account in your name. In five years you will leave my employ a millionaire." Gordon began to hyperventilate. The idea of becoming wealthy at forty-one was overwhelming. With nothing to lose except a nagging wife, bills, and wondering if he'd ever again obtain a decent job, Gordon saw no reason to hedge.

"Ok Mellon, you've got a deal."

After signing the document Pike looked over to Mellon's manservant. "Ok, now what?" With a look of disdain John's eyes darted back to the malevolent employer.

"Go ahead, tell him John." With a deadpanned expression, John revealed Pike's new duties.

"You have seen Mrs. Mellon's playroom. It is mere child's-play against that of Mr. Mellon's." He took Gordon by the arm. "Shall we visit the master's chamber?" He pulled at Gordon's sleeve. "You will be expected to report at eight o'clock each morning." John quickly led him out into the hall. As they walked up the large set of stairs leading to Mellon's private quarters, Gordon flinched. "So what's in store for me up there?"

"Mr. Mellon has a penchant for exploring the limits of a man's endurance." He stopped at the landing. Opening his shirt he showed Pike several old wounds from what looked like piercings. All Pike could imagine was hanging from the ceiling from hooks on chains. Looking into Gordon's eyes he nodded. "Yes, you will work hard for your money and you will pray for the end of each day. If feeling generous, Mellon may grant you a few hours here and there with Mrs. Mellon," he quipped, "just to break the monotony. Believe me, you will wish for a change after a few days with Mellon."

Pike gasped, "So what about the money, was that just a ruse?"

"Oh no, you'll get your money," a smirk briefly crossing his face. "Mellon is a man of his word. He will honor the deal. But you may never live to use your new-found wealth."

Pike swallowed hard. "What do you mean?"

"Many years ago, Mellon acquired a certain book. He told me a great and powerful duke who survived the Spanish Inquisition vowed to use what he had learned from this book against the church and society in general."

"What kind of book?" "A book of Satanic rituals, and from it Mellon found a new use for his money. He used it to bind his will to Satan, an unholy union for preservation and perverted pleasures...and to enslave people, discarding them when finished.

"So, what does that have to do with me?" Pike asked.

"According to the terms, Mellon uses the lore of money and a chance for a new life in return for servitude. He brings people into his employ in a perverse ode to the church's teaching of the seven deadly sins. People like you Pike."

Pike asked, "You mean there are others here who are paid to sin?"

"Yes, there is one presently in the mansion who eats seven meals a day. When he was hired, Mellon asked him what he liked to do most. The man's answer was eating at Mc Donald's. He began his servitude at one hundred-fifty pounds. He now weighs over 600 pounds." Shaking his head, Pike grimaced. "I see...the sin of Gluttony."

"Yes, it has been a most difficult challenge for Mellon's personal chef."

John continued, "There is a self-deluded artist residing in the carriage house. A drunkard now, he paints life-sized nude portraits of Mrs. Mellon. When each is finished, it is burned by Mellon and another immediately commissioned."

"The sin of pride?" he wondered. "Are there others?" Gordon asked.

"Yes, a computer wiz recently finished his private education at the mansion. He is tasked with creating a trading program to swindle wealthy investors...an interesting position to be sure."

"The sin of greed with Mellon the recipient of the profits."

John continued, "An ex-model, long past her prime, resides in a room of mirrors. Having been subjected to three years of grotesque plastic surgeries, she now has only the memories of youth and her original portfolio for consolation."

"Oh, I've got it, Vanity," Pike mused.

"Yes, and so many more," John concluded. "Those who have managed to leave are both scarred and drained of dignity. They wander this world, mere shells of humanity. Several resorted to suicide rather than continue on in shame. Others take it out on society through murder, rape and arson. Do you get the picture now Mr. Pike?"

Gordon slumped in place as John continued.

"You are now a ward of the Mellon's to be used for sex or other sadistic games ginned up for their pleasure. Yours will be the sin of lust."

Gordon blinked hard. "For five years?"

John paused, recounting his own time in service. "Mellon's need to procure willing souls keeps him very busy, that and his wife's insatiable lust for younger men."

"So does anyone ever get out with money?"

"I have been told so, but none with less than five years of service. My signature went on paper over four years ago.

In desperate need a job, I fell into the trap, just as you have, Pike. Now all I can count on is my position and this place to call home." His eyes scanned the massive roof structure above them. "Those who managed to break Mellon's contract are gone, dead souls tormented I suppose in some dark corner of hell."

Gordon shuddered. "Dead souls?"

"Yes, each murdered within days of leaving the grounds. I believe that Mellon had them killed though I've not been able to confirm who he hired to perform the service." John paused for a moment. "I've never wanted to take the chance of leaving the grounds after...."

Gordon grabbed John's shoulder and he winced. "You should have warned me, John." His eyes now burned with an intensity that scared the manservant.

"I didn't expect you to stay, but it seems that the lure of Mellon's money got the best of you. You signed up for the job and now they have you for five years." He paused again surveying Pikes face.

"Gordon, there is no escape. I once tried...got hold of my contract. Mellon caught me with suitcase in hand and the contract stuffed in my jacket. Severely punished, I was warned that the next time, death would follow."

Pike frowned, his mind racing as he processed the information. Now pledged to a crazy old Satanist and his nymphomaniac wife, he thought back to the two prostitutes encountered in the bar - Easy money, he had quipped at the time, servicing strangers for a hundred bucks. Pike's face turned grim. He moved closer to the manservant whispering, "Hell of a way to make a buck!"

"Yes, well, you'll get used to it," John quipped. Sliding over to a display of ancient weapons, Pike pulled a short blade from its sheath and struck. The man-servant fell to the floor, bleeding out from the cut across his jugular. Looking down at his prey, Gordon Pike remarked, "Sorry, but I believe a new job opportunity has opened up and I mean to take it."

Somewhere within the expanse of the mansion laughter echoed as Mellon and his wife celebrated Pike's blood sacrifice. Gordon had proven himself a conscientious hire. Now a murderer, he would serve his master well...until the next resourceful job applicant.

THE END

BLOOD THERAPY

Jason Brandow had been lost. The roads he was traveling were nothing like those in his native land - no signs or landmarks or guardrails to protect the car should it fail to properly navigate the sharp switchbacks. As he travelled up the steep mountainside, the young man searched desperately for signs of life along the road.

Pushing on, Jason became resolute. This was the chance of a lifetime. The late night meeting with the rich benefactor was an opportunity for redemption and could lead to international fame and the wealth. Jason confidently proceeded behind the wheel, up-shifting as he powered his way through the dark and onward toward his destiny. He was late for the appointment but that did not deter him. He felt invigorated by the chance to make his mark. The gears of his BMW whined, as the rental car sailed along the twisting unpaved road toward the remote mountaintop estate of Herr Jurgens."I must be getting close," Jason mumbled to himself. It was very late and he was alone. Looking out to the left, a glimmer of light caught his eye, but quickly disappeared. He stopped the car. Craning for another look up the mountain, he spied light filtering through the trees. "Ayah!" he chortled with glee. The sight of Jurgen's castle reassured the young American doctor that he had arrived.

Although glad to have found the castle, Jason was nearly two hours late. The meeting with Herr Jurgens was a fresh opportunity at redemption. It was also Jason's last chance to perfect the breakthrough procedure that had consumed his every waking moment since graduating medical school. His experiments in tissue regeneration had shown promise, but his careless use of indigent donors put a stop to funding. Censured and removed from the teaching university staff, Jason could not be deterred. He posted the nearly completed findings on the worldwide web. After months with no results, Jason received the unexpected offer of help. It had come from a man with money and power. He wanted to help Jason, provide the money and the equipment to help Jason finish his work.

■■

As he pulled up to the castle gates, Jason felt a sharp pain.

Pressing into his groin area, he let out a groan. His swollen bladder ached. But Brandow couldn't stop, besides there were no rest stops on the tortuous mountainous road leading up to the castle. "I shouldn't have drank those beers," he groused. Jason needed immediate relief. Just a few more minutes he thought, and then...

The large medieval castle stood precipitously at the far edge of the last of three terraced levels. Jason could not wait to explore, but at that moment, nature called for action. Considering the long uphill walk to the entrance, he knew that he could not make it without draining his bladder.

Climbing out of the car, he quickly scooted behind a tree. Hurriedly, Jason unzipped his fly and immediately, a steady stream of urine rushed forth. Halfway to finishing his task, the estate's entry gates opened but pressing on, Brandow groaned. As the flow slowed to a dribble, a distinctively feminine voice called out from the shadows,

"Why do you come to make water on our trees?"

It was a woman's voice, and tugging at his unzipped fly, he sheepishly turned to meet the inquisitor. Dressed in a flowing gown of beautiful white lace, the young woman smiled thinly. She was young, twenty-five he supposed, but waif-like and gaunt. Surprised, his boyish face scrunched up and he apologized.

"Oh, I am sorry. I just couldn't hold it any longer.

She responded more seriously,

"Mine namen... Oh, so sorry, my name is Elsa." Her cold Nordic eyes were dark, like pools of ebony ink, and her skin was a pale pink, nearly transparent in the late autumn moonlight. Elsa's hair fell in long jet-black sterile strands and immediately Jason noticed that it was a poorly fitted wig.

"Well, I take you to Papa. He waits – says to have sent car, but too late. Your hotel says you gone."

"Yes, but perhaps..."

As she grasped his hand her touch was cold. Pulling away, he moved to retrieve his briefcase and turning back, he followed behind as she skipped briskly up the drive.

When they reached the entrance, a large burly manservant appeared. He grabbed Jason tightly by the arm and as the American turned back to Elsa, she breezed past them, disappearing into the shadows. Entranced by the interior's gaudy trappings, Jason's eyes darted about. Slowly, the manservant led him through the open hall to a set of open doors. They then entered into a well lit formal drawing room.

The room's red brocade walls reached down to meet a layer of walnut wainscoting. A small crystal chandelier dispersed its light on several oversized medieval tapestries depicting fierce battle scenes of the crusades. At the far end of the room, a set of wingback chairs fronted a massive fireplace. The smell of tobacco and wood caught his attention and Jason noticed smoke rings and the silhouette of a man tucked into the left-hand chair. The figure stirred but did not get up to greet him.

"Come in Mr. Brandow, I'm happy to finally meet you."

The servant released Jason's arm and quietly retreated from the room. The young man flexed his shoulders. Rubbing at his freed arm, he excused himself.

"I am sorry that your daughter had to... I was..."

"Pissing, yes I know. When you pulled up, she was waiting and rushed out to greet you." Jurgens was a frail man. However, his eyes were devilishly bright. He did not move in the chair, only his head and mouth showed animation. Jason thought that strange but continued,

"I... I am sorry..."

"Don't worry Mr. Brandow, she is a woman of the world. Elsa knows much about life. Don't let Elsa's appearance fool you. She is quite mature." A moment of tense silence followed with a new question from Jurgens.

"Have you brought along your records on skin and nerve regeneration?" His eyes lit up. Smiling widely, Jason's benefactor could not hold back his excitement.

"Why, yes - here." Jason lifted up the briefcase. Suddenly

fixated on his host's toothy grin, thoughts turned to the legend of the undead - vampire. Brandow realized that his host was not an old wealthy industrialists looking for immortality in name only. He obviously wanted Jason's knowledge for some other purpose.

"Excuse me for asking such a pointed question her Jurgens, but what caused you to send for me?"

"Good, you are asking the right questions. A very perceptive young man, handsome and smart." Again, there was a brief silence. Then Jason's host called out, "Elsa, please come.

It is time." Jurgen's face turned somber. "I cannot fight this affliction alone. I may be immortal but the world has changed and with it, the maladies that now cause so much anguish. But Elsa...how impatient she has become."

Elsa came into the room. She removed her hair, a dark flowing wig. Tossing it aside, the wraith's hands came up to her face. Jason watched in horror as Elsa pealed back a paper-thin mask of fresh human skin. She disrobed revealing two heavily desiccated arms and rotting torso. She smiled broadly and her eyes widened. It was then that Jason noticed the two evenly spaced, elongated fangs. Recoiling in shock and revulsion, he stepped back. Suddenly, Jason felt something grabbing him from behind. It was Jurgens. The old vampire arose from his chair and swiftly embraced the doctor. Brandow braced for the inevitable draining of his life's blood. Instinctively, he flinched.

Jurgens released his grip. Turning him around, the benevolent host offered his decrepit hand. Squeezing gently he explained, "I brought you here to help us. We are the last of our breed. As you gathered, we suffer from a deadly infection, a flesh-eating virus that threatens our existence. Doctor, you are our last hope. Everything that you need, including a fresh supply of donors is in the lab below us. Elsa, please show Jason to the laboratory."

"Yes Papa...come doctor, we get started now."

Jason's guts churned, and as the undead maiden led him down to the lab, he could hear the muffled wails of those of whom Jurgens had spoken. Jason Brandow felt a warm sensation running down his left pant leg, his heart pounding from the fear of what lay ahead. Excitedly, Elsa grabbed his arm urging him onward. Stopping half way down the stairway, she offered. "Don't be afraid of death. It is not so bad, especially when you come back as an immortal. If successful, you will become one of us. If not we shall meet our fate together, you and I." She came close, bit her lip and kissed him. Then the vampire took him, the first of many feeds, just a taste of pure and untainted blood.

THE END

THE DIVERSION

I am a hopeless narcissist. Nevertheless, in seeking relief from the reality of a day off without a solid plan, I wandered into an unexplainable happenstance. It was Friday morning in mid- July and after breakfast, I found myself longing for a quick cleanup followed by a mid-afternoon nap. Massive thunderstorms preceded by flashes of lightning had interrupted the previous night's sleep. As now recalled, it may have been a precursor of the strange events that followed.

After two hours of chores I found myself unable to nap and picking up a book, one of Stephen King's latest, I prepared for an entertaining read. Settling into an overstuffed but well-worn black leather recliner, I began to read. Forty-some pages into the dark world of descriptive horror, I put down the book and picked up the TV remote. Clicking the ON button I leaned forward, hoping that visual stimulation might better hold my attention. The video display lasted about ten minutes and as the channels changed, only boorish infomercials, sporting recaps, talk shows, and the like could be found.

Boredom forced my hand. Picking up the phone my finger hit the speed dial for my ex-girlfriend's number. But foolish pride retaliated and quickly I disconnected. She would not come over, even with an honest promise of dinner and a show. She'd say something snide like, "I expect that certain favors would be required for such a monetary investment."

She often said before the break-up, "After all, it's always about you isn't it?"

The television clicked off. Sitting back my eyes closed briefly, tuning only into the sounds of the outside world. A truck came up the drive and I listened as it squealed to a stop. Familiar pneumatic sounds registered in my brain. Without benefit of a clear view I envisioned its giant arm swing down, attacking one of the trash containers lining my street. Feeling the power of the truck's hydraulics, I sensed its great claw pulling the container up and over to deposit its contents into the bowels of the vehicle. I imagined it a living-breathing monster devouring everything in its path along my narrow suburban street. With a bang, the truck dropped the emptied bin and scooted off to its next victim down the line. I laughed at the thought that this diversion so easily held my attention.

I needed a fantasy and my silly little daydream about the

trash truck had re-kindled my desire to get away from reality, if only for a few hours. There was a travel magazine on my coffee table, a complimentary copy recently received with a card offering a two-year subscription. Picking it up, I thumbed through the pages stopping on occasion when something of interest caught my eye. Nearly halfway through the glossy pages

I found my diversion, a beautiful Caribbean beach resort overlooking an expanse of blue sky and crystal clear ocean water. As my eyes focused on the beach, three beautiful women suddenly appeared. Their lithe bodies lay on small grass mats near an oddly shaped thatched roof shelter. One of the beauties was a blonde in a skimpy black two-piece suit; the second a petite redhead wearing a bright green string bikini. The third, a buxom brunette in a mini polka dot micro-bikini held my attention the longest. I imagined myself in the picture, standing on the hot sand in chinos and loafers. Intrigued by my daydream dilemma, I decided to take it a bit further. The brunette would to be the lucky recipient of my attention. She was closest to the strange cone shaped shelter and my thoughts were to get her to join me inside so that I could get to know her better.

Then it happened. Suddenly, I was in the picture. The smell of marine salt filled the air as a mild wind drifted in from the sea. I began to sweat and absent of sunglasses, I squinted to get a better look at the three beach beauties. Noticing me, the brunette picked up her grass mat, smiled, and with a sexy wink, strolled into the thatched cabana.

The other beauties also picked up their mats and paraded down the beach. I could see two shelters farther down. As they reached their respective shelters, each beckoned me to join them.

No, I thought, I was hot for the brunette, and would stick with the first to show interest. Turning back with carnal intentions

I marched to the first cabana and nearing the entrance, my brown loafers slid deep into the soft sand. Falling onto the white-hot surface, I chuckled at my clumsiness. Taking off my shoes and socks, I rolled up my chinos and unbuttoned my long-sleeved cotton shirt.

Sweat was trickling down my neck and onto my chest and I longed for a frosty mug of beer. In my diversion she would be waiting with a cold one just inside the hut. The daydream was now reality and I wanted more. Heat waves danced around the outside of the structure creating a mirage of sensuousness. Thoughts of copper brown skin, swaying hips, and silken brown hair danced in my head.

That was enough to tickle my loins into action. Picking myself up and brushing off the sand I, moved to the doorway. At that moment a new reality took hold. The waking world no longer mattered. In the daydream my body was young and fit with washboard abs, bulging biceps, and classic GQ magazine looks. But there was one constant yet to be considered, my predilection to slow starts and fast finishes. When it came to seduction, one could not wish away a lack of self-confidence in the sack.

What would I say? What could I get away with? The internal questions turned subtle. What would she say or how would she react? Understanding my own limitations, I decided that I'd follow her lead. The diversion had taken complete hold on me. Closing my eyes to the change of light I strolled in.

Once inside they quickly opened. It was dark and steamy with strange musky odors wafting within the dank space. Searching the confines of the shelter proved unsuccessful. She was nowhere to be found. My lips tightened and turning to back to the doorway, I did a double take.

The door had disappeared and the enclosure was now completely sealed. Strong smells of stale beer, spoiled meat and rotten fruit permeated the air within the structure. Gagging from the stench, I placed a shirtsleeve across my nose and mouth.

Moments later the sound of a large diesel truck was heard rolling up next to the enclosure. Placing my ear against the smooth inner-sanctum I listened, but the reverberation within the enclosure stifled clear understanding of what was going on outside. Pounding on the semi-hard surface I yelled, "Hello, anybody...can you hear me? Get me out." There was no response except for the sound of the hydraulics.

"Where are you?" I protested, hoping she would reappear to assist me in my quest for freedom. "She'll help me…then we'll have a few laughs and…" My mind suddenly went blank.

But I was in a dream of my own making. I had fallen into a dream and was in this crazy world of sun and sand and beautiful young women. But the dream was becoming a nightmare of sorts. I was trapped in a hut with nobody around. It was a strange sensation to have no control over this ever-growing feeling of dread.

I decided to just go with it and let this dream play out. As a grown man, I had nothing to fear and it was perfectly fine to let it end with some young wild thing rescuing me from the darkness of despair.

But the diversion was figment of imagination, not a dream. Previous dream related experiences always ended well. I had succumbed to many mid-day dream-like dalliances and conquered every nightmare that came in the night. This situation was very different.

 "Hello, out there, can anyone hear me?" was all I could think to yell, but there was no response. The brunette had led me into this daytime nightmare and the mystery now concerned what would happen next. The heat and stink inside made me sick to my stomach and I could feel bile rising into my throat. Without warning, I heaved onto my shirt; it was a dry heave, disgusting nonetheless with just a few drops of spittle and bile.

As noise from the machinery grew louder, I began searching for another way out. The sides of my new prison suddenly began to expand like a large Tupperware container filled beyond capacity. Control over the diversion now became the chief concern. But there was no time for contemplation. Without warning the enclosure began to shake wildly. Slowly it started to elevate, the sides collapsing as if squeezed it in a great monster's jaws. Losing my balance, I fell back to the floor in a heap of refuse that only enhanced my feelings of dread.

My small prison rose into the air, tilting halfway through its ascent. The roof swung open and everything inside began to shift, myself included. Edging toward the lid I caught a glimpse of the brunette. Sitting in the cab of a large refuse truck, she maneuvered the levers that controlled its massive collection arm. Laughing and wild-eyed, she tossed her silky hair around. As the enclosure reached its apex, my thoughts turned somber. In that moment of self-consciousness, I remembered the sage advice of my mother, "Idle thoughts are the devils playground."

Like in the fairy tale Alice, I became pawn in the wacky world of Wonderland. It was with one subtle change. The subject of the story was now a foolish man chasing after a brunette vixen. I had fallen into an alternate reality of my own making and there seemed no way out. Closing my eyes I imagined the look of disdain on my mother's face. I could hear her voice as she scolded, "Bad boy... you should have chosen a less decedent diversion."

Suddenly, I awoke. The magazine lay on my lap folded open to the bright sandy beach, the blue sky, and wispy clouds dancing around a big yellow sun. There was a hut, its thatched roof hinged open with huge unopened paper umbrellas sticking through the top. A pair of dark skinned men dressed in crisp white linen jackets and black tuxedo pants stood on either side of the entrance. One held a tray of fruity rum drinks and the other a bottle of Jamaican rum in his brilliant white-gloved hands. The tag line of the ad read, "Jamaican Rum, Life's Wonderful Diversion!"

The three beauties were gone and searching in vain, I scoured the scene. Confounded by the experience, I folded the magazine over. On the back cover another photograph caught my eye. There she was, the brunette dressed in orange overalls and showing just enough of her buxom womanhood to make it interesting. Her smiling face augmented by sensuous ruby red lips hovered above a steering wheel in the cab an immaculately appointed refuse truck. The other beauties dressed in blue overalls, posed sensuously at the truck's rear. The ad read:

"CENTENNIAL WASTE INDUSTRIES INC. – PERSONAL SERVICE WITH A SMILE"

Grinning broadly, I flipped the magazine back to its cover.

Soon the light-heartedness turned to bewilderment as I spied the rolled up chinos. A further exploration of my physical condition revealed a strong odor of sweat and bile wafting from the sleeve of my unbuttoned shirt. A pair of loafers and dark cotton socks lay in a heap nearby. Lifting my left leg, it crossed over to the opposite knee. Then in a moment of paranoid disbelief, a fine stream of beach sand fell from between my toes. Swallowing hard, I slumped to the floor frozen in fear. It was a crazy feeling, but once realizing that I was at home, my thoughts turned to every man's elixir of choice.

Tossing the magazine, I ran into the kitchen and threw open the refrigerator door. Grabbing a twelve-pack of Bud light cans, I retired to my front porch and popped a lid. In the fading light of day the first of many quickly emptied. Evening shade was creeping over the rooftops and I wondered how the dream could have lasted so long. After depositing eight cold ones into my gut, sleep overtook me. Empty cans littered the porch like so many dead tin soldiers.

The night passed uneventfully and without so much as a piss break. The beers had chased away any chance for a relapse of the nightmare and I awakened just as dawn began to break. Early morning sounds drifted through the air. Birds began to chirp announcing the coming of a new day; somewhere down the street dogs barked. Humans had not yet made their entrance and I was glad to be alone in my solitude.

As I pulled my aching body off the wooden porch floor, my head began to throb. I looked around at the empty beer cans and counted, four...five...six.... My dream had caused panic and confusion and the price for the retreat into an alcoholic stupor was my hangover. Collecting the empty cans, I balanced them against my chest, the goal to deposit them in my empty trash container.

I reached the curb to deposit the cans, but stopped dead in my tracks as a refuse truck turned the corner. The grinding of its gears only heightened my confusion since my trash pick-up had occurred the previous day. Senselessly panicking, I dropped the cans and fled back to the house. Slamming the front door behind me, I peeked out through the sidelight's sheer curtain. I cringed as the truck bypassed the other houses and slowly made its way to my house. After briefly passing by, the vehicle suddenly stopped. Pausing for a moment, the driver then threw the truck into reverse.

Dressed in an orange jumpsuit open halfway to the waste, the brunette quickly leapt from the cab and began picking up the empties. Throwing the cans into the bin she jumped into the truck and powered up the hydraulics. After dumping the near empty can, she turned her attention to the fool watching her every move. The buxom beauty waved. "I see you made it back." Her wide smile and full set of ruby red lips made my heart skip a few beats. The maven's face glowed brilliantly through the pre-morning mist and her dark brown eyes beckoned with a com-hither look. I wanted to have her right there.

Jostling the front door, I cursed loudly. For no apparent reason it had stuck shut and I twisted and pulled. Now frantic, I believed my chance with her was still a possibility. At last the door popped opened and I passed through just as the truck began pulling away. A cloud of fumes trailed behind covering the impromptu escape.

Feverishly, I ran after that phantom rig and it sped up leaving me to watch as it melted into the pre-dawn morning.

A month had passed since that chance encounter with the women and the trash truck. My world had unexpectedly turned upside down and I wondered each day if it was merely a moment of madness. One thing was certain; my perspective on women changed greatly as a result of the experience. Recently, my ex-girlfriend called. Her greeting was quite disarming.

"Hello honey, I received the sweet friendship card that you sent."

"Card?" I asked apologetically.

"Yes, the funny one with the picture of a man standing in a pile of trash," she replied.

"I laughed at the verse...I'm just trash without you."

My mind began to race and a sudden dread overtook me. She added more seriously, "I thought about the side note and I've decided to give us another chance."

I asked her to elaborate and she paraphrased, "When you wrote that you couldn't get my red lips, silky hair, and beautiful brown eyes off your mind." I did not remember sending that card, but those words drove me to wonderment. After a moment's reflection I unabashedly took credit for the card and the note, a fitting end to a mid-summer diversion, I thought. How wrong I was thinking that I could get away with such a story. But I could not get that girl, the sultry garbage truck driver out of my mind and each night I drempt of her, wanting her, needing to know if she could be real.

That following Saturday Alice came to visit. We had a pleasant evening and when I asked if she planned to stay over she excitedly said,

"Oh, I was hoping you'd ask." She had a small bag in her car and dashed out to retrieve it. As I waited the phone rang.

"Hello," I blurted.

 "Well, are you gonna thank me for sending the card?"

I froze for a minute. The caller was a woman, young and sultry, and I knew that she was the one….the one who had tempted me to carnal fantasy. "Well," she repeated, "Are you gonna thank me or must I come over there."

I clenched my teeth. "No, don't do that," I said. My mind was spinning out of control and in haste I replied, "Thank you for sending the card....now go away."
I heard the phone click and she was gone.

Wiping my sweaty brow, I only hoped that my crazy dream was just that. After all, I could not have had the experience of dreaming up a woman who happened to be a nut-job ready to mess up a good thing between my girl and I. The next thing I heard was a loud crash just outside. Running to the window, I spied a large garbage truck careening down the street. It had plowed right into my girlfriend's car, leaving it a mess of smashed metal and plastic.

"Alice!" I screamed. Making my way down the front steps I saw her slumped over the front seat. A neighbor had seen the accident and began to pull her from the wreckage. Running from the house to her lifeless body, I realized that it was too late: she was dead. Then I noticed the open note on the front seat. It read,

Thanks for taking good care of our boy but he's all mine now.

From inside the house I heard the phone ring. Somehow I knew that it was the girl in the truck.

THE END

The Underground Passage

The spelunker acted alone

against what cooler heads

would have duly cautioned

through ardent protestation.

As he made the descent

into the bowels of the earth

faint rumbles came forth

from within that cavern.

By rope and angled spike

he repelled ledge that ledge

until the artful dodge settled

at the base of the cave.

Too late his welcome soured

as menacing groans from above

shattered all hope of ascent

to the entrance and freedom.

Soiled by momentary terror

the explorer chose a path

down a long narrow cut

deep into the mountain's gut.

Pausing for a moments rest

he spied a dim orb of light

flickering faintly in the dark

beyond his narrow beam.

Buoyed by a chance to exit

he forged ahead in earnest

certain of impending doom

should he tarry back too long.

Onward in darkness he trekked

along a natural stone bridge

through a long arched tunnel

that led to a massive stone hall.

Sitting on a great golden throne

the lord of the underworld

hailed his unexpected guest

and bade him enter within.

Massive doors closed from behind

and with a clap of his hands

the lord sealed off the rift above

entombing the explorer forever.

E.W. Bonadio

AFTERWARD

We hope that these stories have entertained, shocked, humored, and most of all, dispelled any notion that everything that can be written has been written.. Unique tales handed down from verbal or written accounts have morphed into new or updated tales garnered from the legends of old. The stories in this anthology are simple windings from the mind of one who likes to create variations on those legends and unexplained happenings of old.

Although the writer is fond of thrillers and paranormal novels, his penchant for dreaming up strange and varied story lines with brevity of words and character development, leaves the reader open to expanding the tale through WHAT-IF endings.

For centuries, man has conjured up spooky stories to delight, excite and confound those who choose to enter the world of dark images and imagination. With electronic publication becoming more prevalent, a good print book still makes sense. As with any book that might prove worthy, it should be passed down to others who share the love of dark passages.

ABOUT THE AUTHOR:

E.W. Bonadio was born in Baltimore, Maryland, the adopted home of Edgar Allan Poe whose works inspire both style and pace in the author's writings. Bonadio has published two novels, a book of poetry, and numerous short stories some of which have placed or have won in literary competitions. His first novel 'Voices', published in 2000, served as the impetus for later works.

Other published works include a children's fantasy book and a humorous memoir. His last thriller novel titled 'The Masada Stones' was published in late 2008. The author recently turned to short story work, two released in print magazines during 2010. Several of his short stories appear in and print editions of Abandoned Towers, Hungur Magazine, Panic Press 2010 anthology, and Soup for Souls. Additional author information is available on web site:

www.ebonadio.com

Printed in Great Britain
by Amazon

19837420R00092